"**Hannah, we need to get out of here. Now!**" Layke's baritone voice boomed with undeniable urgency.

"What's going on?"

"Propane leak and our position has been compromised."

She ushered Gabe down the hall to where Layke had the front door open and was waiting.

Layke nudged her out the door. "Come on!"

"Where will—"

An explosion cut off her words and rocked the cabin's structure, propelling the trio off the front porch. They fell into a mound of snow.

Layke jumped up and dragged her and Gabe farther down the laneway.

A second blast turned the cabin into a fireball and slammed a gush of heat in their direction as debris pelted them.

Layke shoved Gabe toward her and used his body to shield both of them.

Gabe cried and squirmed in an attempt to get out from under them.

Layke jumped up and lifted the boy into his arms. "Get to the car! Run, Hannah!"

Darlene L. Turner is an award-winning author who lives with her husband, Jeff, in Ontario, Canada. Her love of suspense began when she read her first Nancy Drew book. She's turned that passion into her writing and believes readers will be captured by her plots, inspired by her strong characters and moved by her inspirational message. Visit Darlene at www.darlenelturner.com, where there's suspense beyond borders.

Books by Darlene L. Turner

Love Inspired Suspense

Border Breach
Abducted in Alaska

ABDUCTED IN ALASKA

DARLENE L. TURNER

LOVE INSPIRED SUSPENSE

INSPIRATIONAL ROMANCE

LOVE INSPIRED® SUSPENSE
INSPIRATIONAL ROMANCE

ISBN-13: 978-1-335-40511-1

Abducted in Alaska

Copyright © 2021 by Darlene L. Turner

PLEASE RECYCLE
THIS PRODUCT IS RECYCLABLE

Recycling programs
for this product may
not exist in your area.

This edition published by arrangement with Harlequin Books S.A.

For questions and comments about the quality of this book, please contact us at CustomerService@Harlequin.com.

Love Inspired
22 Adelaide St. West, 40th Floor
Toronto, Ontario M5H 4E3, Canada
www.Harlequin.com

Printed in U.S.A.

I will praise thee; for I am fearfully and
wonderfully made: marvellous are thy works;
and that my soul knoweth right well.

My substance was not hid from thee,
when I was made in secret, and curiously wrought
in the lowest parts of the earth.

Thine eyes did see my substance, yet being unperfect;
and in thy book all my members were written,
which in continuance were fashioned,
when as yet there was none of them.
—*Psalm* 139:14-16

For Murray (Murly-the-Whurly), my amazing brother
I miss you

ONE

Border patrol officer Hannah Morgan stepped through the doors of the Canadian Services Border Agency station in Beaver Creek, Yukon. Strong winds assaulted her exposed face, but she didn't mind. It would help take away the sting of the recent news she'd received. Well, if that was possible. The blinding snow pelted her as she trudged from under the station's covered border crossing.

Movement at the tree line caught her eye, jarring her from the winter conditions. What was that? She pulled her flashlight from her pocket and shone it toward the woods. A young boy emerged from the tree cover, stumbling through the blizzard…coatless. He fell face-first into the deep fresh-fallen snow.

Hannah yelled and raced toward the boy. She had to reach him and fast. Who knew how long he'd been out in the elements? Frostbite would set in soon—if it hadn't already.

It took her only seconds to reach him. She pulled him out of the powdery mess. His matted curly hair held embedded chunks of snow, revealing hints of brown mixed with white. Hannah guessed him to be about seven or eight.

He whimpered, his teeth chattering through bluish lips. She had to get him inside. Now.

"I've got you." She pulled off her CBSA-issued parka

and wrapped it around him. "Here, this will help." She ignored the biting wind that whipped through her long-sleeved shirt. His safety was her only concern.

"He's. After. Me." The boy's words stumbled out in shivering whispers.

"Who's after you?"

Movement from the tree line answered her question. Once again, she shone her flashlight. A man scrambled through the woods, a gun at his side. He spotted them and raised his weapon, revealing his intention. He wanted the boy.

Hannah grabbed the boy's hand. "Run!" she yelled. With her free hand, she unleashed her Beretta. Not that she could fire well in the disappearing daylight, but she needed to be prepared. She would not let harm come to this boy. Not on her watch.

They raced across the field, ploughing through the snowstorm. Tightness attacked her chest as her airways constricted. No! Her asthma couldn't flare up now. Not when someone else was in danger. She breathed in deeply and veered the boy toward the border patrol station.

A shot rang out, echoing in the area as snow sprayed them from the bullet gone wide. *God, protect us.*

The boy stumbled on a fallen branch. She stuffed her weapon back into its holster, lifted him in her arms and kept running. Another shot pierced the night. Hannah raced in a zigzag pattern, determined not to give the shooter an easy target. Even though the boy was light-weight, her arms became heavy from carrying him. She ignored the discomfort and concentrated on one thing.

Reaching the station and safety.

A shadow emerged ahead under the building's light in the now darkened area.

Her boss.

He had heard the shots.

"Run, Hannah!" He raised his weapon, ready to fire.

She was almost at the border patrol station.

Another shot rang out, hitting the light and plunging the dusk into darkness. A coyote howled in the distance. She knew they ran in packs, but the gunfire should keep them away.

She stumbled, then caught her footing as she reached the roadway.

"Hurry," her boss shouted, racing toward them.

Within seconds, Superintendent Doyle Walsh reached them and grabbed the boy from her. "Quick, into the station." The older officer's father-like tendencies had comforted her throughout her career with the CBSA. They were safe with him.

She whipped open the door and held it for her boss and the boy. She slammed it shut, locking it.

A gush of heat embraced her like a brick wall of safety. How long would it hold before the assailant breached it?

"We have to brace the doors." Hannah began to push a short filing cabinet in front of the door. Hopefully, it would at least give them some protection. "Help me." Her shallow breathing stole her air. She breathed in and out slowly to calm her racing heart.

Doyle set the boy in a chair and helped her shove the cabinet across the floor.

A bullet struck the window.

Hannah lunged for the boy, pulling him onto the floor. "Get down!"

More bullets struck the building, but the bulletproof glass held.

Shouts sounded from outside. The assailant had called in reinforcements.

Who were these people and why were they after the boy?

When no more shots came, she eased herself up and

glanced out the window. A man with spiked hair appeared within inches of the building, staring directly at her. His cold eyes personified evil and he sneered. He raised his cell phone and pressed it against the glass. A picture of her on Facebook appeared. *What?* His intent was clear. He knew her identity and she was now a target.

Hannah stumbled backward, falling to the floor, and pulled out her inhaler. *Lord, keep my asthma at bay.* She put her lips on the mouthpiece, took a puff and then exhaled to still the panic threatening to overpower her body. How did he know who she was in such a short time?

The boy cried beside her.

She gathered him into her arms. With the unexpected news from her doctor only an hour ago indicating she would probably never bear a child of her own, she had the sudden urge to protect this boy. "You're safe with us. Are you hurt?"

He shivered in her embrace and shook his head. How long had he been out in the cold?

"What's your name?" Doyle knelt beside them.

The curly-haired boy hiccuped through his tears. "Gabe."

His chocolate-brown eyes reminded Hannah of a puppy dog. Her heart melted. "How old are you?"

He raised eight white-tipped fingers.

Hannah smiled before wrapping her hands around his tiny ones. She needed to warm him up. "What's your last name, Gabe?"

"Stewart."

Shouts alerted her to the continued danger outside.

"Did you call 911?" Hannah asked her boss.

Doyle nodded. "They should arrive any moment now."

The station's phone trilled and he hit the speaker button. "Beaver Creek Station."

"Give up the boy and we might let you live," the deep voice growled.

Gabe whimpered.

Hannah held him tighter. *Lord, bring reinforcements now!* The normally peaceful small station housed only a couple of officers. They were outnumbered.

Flashing lights lit up the area as sirens pierced the night. Her prayer was answered.

More shots rang out.

She eased up and peeked out the window. Lights bounced from tree to tree as gunfire pierced through the inky sky. Gabe's sobs reminded her of the need to keep the boy from harm. She had to get him safely out of the station. How, with the assailants so close?

A police constable crouched behind his cruiser with his weapon raised.

He fired and glanced toward the station, the sole remaining streetlight revealing his features.

Where had she seen him before? She searched her memory and couldn't come up with the answer.

Machine gun fire peppered the window.

She screamed and fell back down on the floor.

Gabe raced to her and latched his arms around her neck, holding her in a vise grip. "Don't let them get me."

His whispered words tore at her heart.

A tear leaked down her cheek as determination surfaced.

She would not let this boy down.

Canadian police constable Layke Jackson cowered behind the cruiser, raising his Maglite and Smith & Wesson in the direction of the shots fired. The dark five-o'clock hour hid the number of assailants lurking in the distance, making it impossible to get a clear line of sight. The wind snaked down his neck, adding to the trepidation creeping into his body. He hated winter. He'd take the beach over mountains any day. He zipped up his jacket tighter to his neck and focused on the task at hand.

Local Beaver Creek constables pulled up beside him. They jumped from their cruiser and flanked him with their weapons raised, protecting the occupants of the station. Layke identified himself over the howling wind.

He had been on his way from Whitehorse hours ago to investigate strange child abductions in the Beaver Creek area when he heard the desperate 911 call from the patrol station. On loan to the Yukon authorities from Alberta, he'd requested to lead the joint task force of a child labor smuggling ring happening along the Yukon-Alaskan borders. He'd jumped at the chance after he received a frantic call from his newly discovered half brother, Murray. His son had mysteriously disappeared and with the high rise of child labor in the area, Layke knew it couldn't be a coincidence. Once his boss and the local corporal approved it, he'd hopped on a plane and headed to Whitehorse.

He promised Murray he'd find his son, Noel. Before it was too late.

Was the boy barricaded in the CBSA station connected to the other abducted children or a coincidence? Could the boy lead them to Noel?

Bullets whizzed over Layke's head, snapping him from his thoughts.

Multiple muzzle flashes revealed the shooters' location.

Layke and the other constables fired in that direction.

When no other flashes erupted, he lowered his weapon. "Hold your fire!"

Silence hushed the night, stilling the wind.

Layke eased himself up, being careful not to make himself a target. "They're gone. Can you secure the perimeter? I'll check on the occupants in the station."

The local constables glanced at each other, then back

to him. One stepped forward. "Where are you from, Constable? Clearly not from around here." His lips flattened.

Oops. Had Layke overstepped his bounds?

He stuck out his gloved hand. "Sorry, I should start over. I'm Constable Layke Jackson on loan from Alberta. You are?"

The fortysomething black-haired constable shook his hand. "I'm Constable Antoine and this is Constable Yellowhead. Why are you in our area?"

"There's reason to believe the boy inside could be one of the recently abducted children. I'm leading a joint task force to capture the child smugglers."

The other constable crossed his arms. "But why from Alberta? Local constables could lead this task force. After all, we know the area better."

Layke had to tread lightly. He couldn't get on their bad side. He needed their help and he also had to get inside to check on the occupants. "Understood. I've had lots of experience in the uptick of child labor smuggling rings across the country. I volunteered to come here." No need to go into all his reasons.

Constable Antoine reached for his radio. "We'll call it in. Then we'll scour the area for the shooters."

Layke pinched his lips together. They were wasting time and the assailants were getting away. However, they were correct. They had to go by protocol. Everything must be done right. Airtight investigations led to solid convictions. It was the way he operated.

He pointed to the station. "I'll check on the CBSA officers and boy inside. Nice meeting you."

They nodded and stepped toward their cruiser.

Layke rushed to the entrance and tried the door. Locked. He banged on it. "Constable Jackson here. Can you open up?"

"Is it safe?" a female's voice yelled from inside.

"Yes. They're gone." At least that appeared to be the case.

He heard scraping sounds, as if the station's occupants were moving furniture. Perhaps they had shoved something in front of the door to protect themselves. Smart thinking.

Moments later, the door eased opened slightly and a blue-eyed CBSA officer peered through the crack. Wiry red hair poked out from under her tuque. "Can you show me some identification?"

He fished out his credentials and held them up. "Can you let me in? It's freezing out here." His tone conveyed a mix of annoyance and authority. Probably not a good first impression, but he was losing his patience. Not his best trait.

She scowled and opened the door wider. "Yes, sir!"

He swept by her and brushed the snow off his jacket. "Everyone good?"

He spied the boy huddled in the corner under a mound of blankets, his body shaking. He rushed over and knelt beside him. "Hey, bud. You okay?"

The boy remained silent.

Layke turned to the officer. "You are?"

"Border patrol officer Hannah Morgan." She pointed to the man on his cell phone. "That's Superintendent Doyle Walsh. He's reporting the incident to our superiors."

Layke stood and pulled out his notebook. "Can you tell me what happened?"

Hannah removed her hat, revealing her disheveled red locks. She tugged at the elastic in her hair and repositioned it. "I was performing a sweep of the area at dusk since the traffic was light when I caught movement at the tree line. Gabe here came through the woods without a coat on."

No wonder he still shivered. How long had he been out in the cold?

"I rushed over and put my jacket around him," Hannah

continued. "He barely told me what was going on when I saw a man with a gun emerge from the trees, rushing at us. I grabbed Gabe's hand and we ran toward the building. The man fired some shots that went wide. Thankfully, God protected us."

God? Hardly. He held his tongue and waited for her to continue.

"My boss heard the shots and came outside. We reached the station and barricaded ourselves in. One of the assailants called us and demanded we release the boy or they'd kill us."

"Any recognizable voice traits? Accent?"

"None, but I won't forget it. It was deep and chilling." She rubbed her arms as if warding off the threat.

"Do you know anything about Gabe?"

"Only that he's eight."

"Any signs of how long he was out in the cold?"

"His fingertips are frostbitten. I treated him."

Gabe held up his bandaged hands.

Layke smiled, pulled up a chair beside the boy and tousled his curls. "Can you tell me why you didn't have a coat on, Gabe?"

He shrugged. "No time. I ran."

"From where?"

A fat tear surfaced and the boy looked at Hannah.

She rushed to his side. "It's okay, Gabe. You can tell Constable Jackson. You're safe now."

"They said they'd kill us."

She rubbed the tear away with her thumb. "Who said that?"

"The bad men."

Layke had to get this boy to trust him. He pulled out his badge and handed it to him. "See this, Gabe? I'm a police officer and I will keep you safe. I promise."

Could he?

Hannah reached for the boy's hand. "We both will."

The station's phone rang, its loud ring booming throughout the small room.

The boy startled.

Hannah jumped up and grabbed the receiver. "Beaver Creek Station." She waited and held it out to Layke. "It's him again. He wants to talk to you."

He stood and walked over to the desk. "Constable Jackson here."

"We know who you are," the baritone voice growled.

What? Layke tugged at his jacket's collar in response to the heat from the small room and the unnerving call. How did they know his name?

"Release the boy or your nephew dies."

Layke stiffened.

Click.

He peered out the window into the night.

The kidnappers were still out there and watching.

Layke's chest constricted as his pulse thrashed in his head, reminding him of a ticking clock. He needed to solve this case before more innocent children were taken, or worse…

He would not allow one hair on their heads to be harmed.

Even if it was the last thing he did.

TWO

Hannah noted the color drain from Constable Jackson's face and his body straighten, his crystal blue eyes widening. The person on the other end of the line had him rattled and she knew why. It was the same caller from earlier and the constable's expression told her they meant business. Whoever *they* were.

She grabbed his arm. "What is it?"

He dropped the receiver back into its cradle and moved her away from the boy. "They somehow know who I am and they have my nephew. They're demanding we release Gabe or they'll kill Noel." His whispered voice held an urgency to it.

Superintendent Walsh clicked off his cell phone and moved to the group, extending his hand. "Constable, I'm the head of this station. I've just learned of your task force. Can you tell us what's going on?"

The constable grasped Doyle's hand. "Layke Jackson. Have you heard of the child labor smuggling ring happening in your area?" He kept his voice low.

"Inklings of it. Share with us what you know, Constable." Doyle removed a notebook from his vest pocket.

"Call me Layke. I'm stationed in Calgary and have been investigating child-smuggling rings occurring across the country."

A lightbulb moment hit Hannah. That's where she'd seen his face. His reports, along with his picture, had been shared through interagency channels. She'd read his findings and respected his attention to detail on the subject. His communications held ample information on the rings. "I read your reports, but why are you here in the Yukon when there are many rings in other areas?" She had heard rumblings of some abductions a few months ago but nothing recent. She thought the threat had passed. What had changed?

He shifted his stance and hooked his thumbs into his pant loops. "Honestly? My nephew Noel was kidnapped two days ago."

Doyle raised a brow. "So it got personal for you."

"Yes. As soon as my half brother called, I had my leader contact Whitehorse's superintendent and he then got in touch with the corporal here. They agreed to allow me to lead the task force because of my research."

"How many rings are there across the country?" Doyle asked.

"Counting this one? Probably four or five, but we don't know how far they reach."

Hannah's mouth dropped open and she gazed at Gabe. The boy had fallen asleep under the cozy blankets. Questions filled her mind. How long had he been held captive? How many other children had this ruthless gang taken? Realization punched her in the gut. She couldn't have children of her own, but she needed to find these young ones. Their innocence had been stolen, and she'd do everything she could to bring them back to their families. She turned to the men. "I want on this task force, Doyle."

Doyle's mustache twitched as he frowned.

Although he treated her like a daughter, she wouldn't let that stand in her way. He had trained her well. She could do this.

She *had* to do this.

"You know I'm capable," she said.

He raked his fingers through his hair. "I know, but I want you to be safe. These men have already proved they're dangerous. You were almost shot earlier."

Layke pointed to Gabe. "And they won't stop until the boy is back with them."

"I can do this. Stopping smugglers is what I'm trained to do. Plus, I'm top at the shooting range. We need border patrol officers on this force," Hannah said.

Doyle sighed. "She's right and she has a heart for children." He stepped closer to her and took his hands in hers. "You'll make a great mother one day."

She snapped backward, his words sucking the life out of her. If he only knew. She'd not only lost her hope for a child but her identity. *God, who am I if I'm not who I want to be the most in this life?* A mother.

His softened eyes showed concern. "What is it, little one?"

His term of endearment.

She wasn't ready to share. "I just want these kids to be safe."

"Fine. The chief of operations has approved me to release an officer to work with the police. I choose you." He took her hands in his again. "Please promise me you'll be careful."

"Of course. You trained me well."

Doyle turned to Layke, poking him in the chest. "And you best keep her safe."

"Yes, sir. I'll take good care of her."

Hannah tilted her head. "I can take care of myself. How else do you think I've survived in this rough terrain? Yukon is not for the faint of heart."

Layke shoved his hands in his pockets. "I didn't mean—"

His radio crackled. "Constable Jackson, this is Constable Antoine." The man's voice came through the speaker. "We've secured the perimeter. No sign of the assailants."

"Copy that," Layke said. "Meet us at your detachment. We'll transport the boy there. It's safer. This place is too out in the open."

"Agreed."

Hannah eyed Gabe. As he slept, his contorted face told her bad dreams plagued him. A wave of anguish washed over her as determination rose throughout her body. She couldn't let him out of her sight. She would protect him at all costs. She turned to Layke. "You're not going to give him over to the gang, are you?"

Layke's eyes clouded. "Of course not. I can't trade one life for another even if it is my nephew. We need to find out more from Gabe. Maybe he can lead us to where they're being held."

"Yes. Perhaps this can be over quickly." Did she really believe that? Nothing to do with crime was ever simple. "I'm going with you."

"Superintendent Walsh, can you release her to the task force now?" Layke asked.

Doyle pulled out his cell phone. "Yes. I will man the station until I can call in a replacement. Now, can you tell us what we're up against? Do you know anything about the Yukon gang?"

"Not a lot yet. If they're like the others I've investigated, they'll be ruthless."

"What do these gangs want with them?" Hannah asked.

"Child labor."

Doyle texted and shoved the phone back into his pocket. "What type?"

"Clothing sweat shops, shoe assembly, farm work. Probably others."

Hannah's stomach roiled as tightness settled in her

chest. These gangs must be stopped. Many children's lives were at stake. "Do we know where they're getting these kids?"

"Each gang is different. We don't know anything about the Yukon one yet."

"So you don't have anything other than Gabe to go on?" Doyle peered out the window.

"No, this is our first lead."

The station's phone rang, stilling the conversation.

Hannah raced to pick it up before it woke Gabe. Her muscles tensed. Could it be the same caller again? "Beaver Creek Station."

"This is Cynthia Simon from child services. I hear you have a young boy in custody."

She sucked in a breath. How did they find out about Gabe so quickly?

"Yes. What can I do for you?"

"He needs to be released to us. Now." Her curt voice held authority.

Hannah stumbled backward.

She couldn't let him go.

Not with his life on the line.

Layke rushed to Hannah's side and caught her before she fell. Their gaze locked for a brief second. Her widened eyes revealed fear. Why? He grabbed the phone from her hand. Could it be the same caller again? "This is Constable Jackson. Who's calling?"

"Cynthia Simon from child services. We need to pick up the boy you have there."

Was it possible this woman was somehow linked to the gang? How else would she know Gabe was there? He would not let the boy go that easily. "Ma'am, he's in police custody and needs to be questioned. Can I ask how you know about this child?"

She cleared her throat. "An anonymous tip from a concerned citizen."

What citizens were around this secluded station? He wasn't buying it. Did the gang think it would be easier to abduct the boy again if Gabe was in the custody of child services? They knew Layke wouldn't turn him over, so they called in the tip.

Hannah pulled at his sleeve, her eyes wild.

"I need to put you on hold, Ms. Simon." He pushed the hold button. "What is it, Hannah?"

"We can't release him. He'll only be safe with us. We need to convince her of that." She chewed on her lip.

Doyle stepped forward. "Can we do that? Don't we have to let him go?"

Could they hold Gabe? What was the protocol for something like this? He was a stickler for the rules. "We probably can't legally hold him."

Hannah sank into a chair. "You have to convince them. I don't care what the proper chain of command is. We need to protect this boy, and my gut is telling me he won't be safe with child services. Please?"

Her gut? He prided himself on following guidelines and not relying on his instincts, as he'd been burned before. Images flooded his mind of a female victim. A woman who not only betrayed him but died under his watch.

One case where he'd trusted his so-called gut. He wouldn't make that mistake again.

He pushed the picture from his mind and concentrated on the conversation.

"Please, Layke. Listen to her," Doyle said. "I trust Hannah."

Layke was outnumbered, and it wasn't that he didn't want the boy safe. He just needed to do things by the book. "Fine."

He clicked back on the call. "Ms. Simon, this boy needs

to stay in police protection. His life is in danger and you can't guarantee he'll be safe with you."

Silence.

He caught her attention.

A sigh sailed through the phone. "Okay, Constable. I'll let my superiors know this is the case. He can stay with you. For now."

He winced. They might have a fight on their hands later if they didn't find this gang soon. "Thank you."

"We'll be in touch." She hung up.

He lowered the receiver into the cradle. "She's letting us keep Gabe. We need to get him to the detachment though. He's not secure here." He eyed the sleeping boy. He appeared so peaceful. Could Layke disturb him? He had to get him out of here.

Hannah jumped up and peered out the window. "Is it safe out there? From the phone call you received from the gang, it sounded like they were watching."

"The constables did a thorough sweep of the perimeter. We'll be fine." Even though he hoped so, he would still take all precautions when moving the boy to his cruiser.

The border patrol officers were trained in firearms, so Layke could rely on their protection. However, he would check out the surroundings before moving the boy. "Stay here. I'll canvass the area around the building before moving Gabe. Hannah, maybe you can get him ready."

She nodded.

He stepped outside the station and into the biting wind. He zipped his jacket closer to his chin and edged toward the side of the building. One remaining streetlight still shone as a beacon in the darkness. Relentless snow continued to hammer the region. Living in Calgary accustomed him to snowy winters, but the shortened daylight in the Yukon, along with the deep cold, only added to his dislike of this season. How did people do it around here?

He pulled out his Maglite, shrugged off thoughts of the frigid weather and moved around the station, shining the beam toward the woods. Stillness greeted him. He circled the building to ensure no one lurked in the shadows, and came up empty. Satisfied they were alone, he pulled out his cell phone, called the Beaver Creek detachment and asked for Constable Antoine.

"How can I help you, Constable Jackson?" His tone conveyed irritation.

What had he done to get on the man's bad side?

"We're bringing the boy in and need a room to keep him safe. Can you get one ready? Something that won't make him feel uncomfortable?"

"We'll arrange it with our corporal."

The snow pellets blinded Layke and he tugged his hat farther down. "Corporal Bakker?"

"Yes, you've met?"

"Not officially, but the sergeant in Whitehorse put me in touch with him."

"Good. You leaving now?"

A rustling from the trees interrupted the night's serenity. Layke stiffened and shone his light in the direction of the sound. Movement caught his attention as a chill tingled his spine.

Was someone still watching them?

Seconds later, two beady eyes appeared through the tree line.

A coyote skulked from the woods.

Layke released the breath he'd been holding and chastised himself for being jumpy. He opened the station's door and stepped inside, brushing the snow off his jacket with his free hand. "Yes, just secured the perimeter again and going to get him into the cruiser along with the CBSA officer who helped him. He seems to trust her."

"See you soon." He hung up.

Layke shoved his cell phone back into his pocket and moved toward Hannah. "Everything is quiet outside. Is Gabe all set?"

She wrapped another blanket around the boy. "Ready to go see a police station, Gabe?"

He rubbed his sleepy eyes. "Really?"

Layke squatted to be at the boy's level. "Yes. I have more officers I want to introduce you to."

"Cool. Will there be bad guys there?"

"Don't worry, we'll keep you safe." He hoped any prisoners at the detachment would be locked behind bars so they wouldn't scare Gabe. He stood and turned to Doyle. "Can you stay close to us on our way to the cruiser?"

"Sure." He pulled out his gun. "Let's go."

"Stay behind me, Hannah." Layke removed his 9 mm but kept it at his side. No need to alarm the boy. "Head to the Suburban quickly."

"Will do." Hannah grabbed Gabe's hand and moved into position.

The group stepped outside into the night and rushed to the vehicle.

Doyle stood close, flanking them.

Layke opened the passenger side and back doors. He pulled Gabe from Hannah's hold and sat him in the front. "How would you like to ride shotgun in a police car?"

The boy's eyes widened. "Yippee!"

"Just don't touch any buttons, okay, sport?"

Gabe tucked his hands under his legs. "Yup."

Hannah chuckled from the back seat, tugging at Layke's heart. He could get used to that sound. Where had that thought come from? He'd vowed not to allow a woman to get close to him again.

Not after what his mother had done to him. His trust factor was low when it came to women. Especially after one he'd been interested in tried to discredit him and damage his reputation.

He fastened Gabe's seat belt, steering his thoughts from the beautiful redheaded officer. "Let's go." He rushed around the cruiser and shook Doyle's hand. "Appreciate your help."

"Anytime. Stay safe." The superintendent waited for him to get into the driver seat and start the engine before he returned to the safety of the station.

Layke peered at Gabe. "You ready, sport?"

He nodded.

Layke backed the cruiser out from the station's parking lot. The snow had subsided to occasional fat flakes, but the road conditions hadn't improved and they fishtailed after pulling onto the highway. He straightened the vehicle and gained control as his cell phone rang. Corporal Elias Bakker's number appeared on the Suburban's dashboard.

Layke hit the talk button. "Corporal, what's up?"

"Constable Jackson, I know you're on your way here, but I need to warn you."

Layke steeled his jaw and glanced at Gabe. The boy seemed interested only in staring at the buttons on the console.

"About what, Corporal Bakker?"

"We've been watching the dark web. There's chatter about a ransom to catch a boy being moved from the Beaver Creek border. Watch your back."

He looked in the rearview mirror. No tail. "Thanks for the—"

A snowmobile lurched onto the highway at high speed, cutting them off.

Layke strengthened his grip on the wheel. Had the assailant hidden in the shadows?

THREE

Hannah jerked back as the snowmobile driver pulled in front of them. The passenger turned and pointed a machine gun in their direction. Hannah yelled, "Gun! Get down!" She pushed Gabe forward in an attempt to protect him from the impending danger. Her motherly instinct took over and all she could think about was the safety of the boy in the front seat. *Lord, keep us safe.* Her breaths came in shallow bursts as her heart thudded in anticipation of a crash. She knew police officers were trained in emergency driving tactics, but her fight-or-flight response took over and she clutched the armrest with her free hand.

Layke swerved the wheel and the Suburban spun before he regained control and headed in the opposite direction.

The snowmobile followed in pursuit, its headlight bouncing behind them. It veered right, revved its engine, and jumped into the field.

"Gabe and Hannah, stay down," Layke said.

"Constable! You still there?" The corporal's voice boomed through the Bluetooth speaker. "Layke, talk to me."

"Send your officers to our location on the AlCan Highway," Layke said. "We're under attack. Assailants on a snowmobile."

"Word got out faster than anticipated. Constables are en route." The call disappeared from the dashboard.

Hannah peeked out the window to find the snow-mobile's location. It raced alongside them at even speed. She pounded the back of the seat. "Faster. They're trying to cut us off again."

The Suburban swerved, then sped up in an attempt to outrun the beast beside them.

"How can I lose him? Is there another road to take?" Layke asked.

"Not really, there's only—"

Gunfire cracked the windshield.

Gabe screamed.

"Stay down, sport!" Layke once again slowed and yanked the wheel right. They fishtailed and swung around in the opposite direction, back toward Beaver Creek.

The assailants turned to follow.

Flashing lights approached in the distance. Two cruisers headed toward them.

The snowmobile turned and sped across the field, disappearing into the night. They gave up the chase.

For now.

Even in the darkened vehicle, Hannah noted Layke's tightened jaw. They were all now targets, and she knew the danger would be relentless if this gang wanted Gabe back. They would definitely try again. Who were *they* and why the interest in Gabe?

Layke slowed and pulled to the side of the road.

The constables stopped and jumped out of their vehicles.

Layke lowered the window. "Thank you for getting here quickly. They took off in that direction." He pointed. "I'm sure they're long gone now."

"I'll scour the area," Constable Yellowhead said, returning to his vehicle.

Constable Antoine waved to Hannah. "Officer Morgan, good to see you again. Sorry it's under bad circumstances."

"Yes. Close call." Hannah rested her hand on Gabe's shoulder. "You okay, bud?"

No answer. His silence told Hannah he was not okay.

Constable Antoine thumped the driver's door. "Let's get you to the detachment. You're sitting ducks out here. Follow me."

Moments later, Layke pulled into the detachment's tiny parking lot. "Stay alert. We can't take any risks with this heightened threat." His stark tone personified authority.

Gabe whimpered.

"You're scaring him," Hannah whispered.

"Let's go," Layke said, ignoring her comment.

They stepped out of the vehicle and Hannah took Gabe's hand. "We need to hurry, bud."

A gray-haired constable held the door. "Welcome to the Beaver Creek Detachment. Good to see you again, Hannah." He turned to Layke. "I'm Corporal Bakker. Nice to meet you face-to-face, Constable."

Layke nodded. "You too, Corporal. Where can we set up?"

He gestured down the short hall. "Our lunchroom. It's tiny but will work. Last door on the right."

Hannah stomped the snow off her boots. "Thanks, Elias."

A thin older woman wearing a bright orange dress with clunky accessories approached. She grabbed Layke's hand. "I'm Martha Bakker, the corporal's wife. I help out here from time to time."

Hannah loved to visit and have tea with Martha on occasion. The woman had a style all her own. The residents of Beaver Creek referred to her as the town's mayor even though she wasn't. She just knew everything about everyone.

Martha knelt in front of Gabe. "You can call me Gramma Bakker. All the kids do. You hungry?" She held out a package of Twizzlers.

Gabe took them. "Thank you."

She stood and squeezed his shoulder. "You're welcome, sweetie. Let's go to the lunchroom, shall we?" She reached out her hand.

The boy hesitated and glanced at Hannah.

"It's okay, Gabe. We're right behind you." It was clear to Hannah that the boy had trust issues, and she couldn't blame him after what he'd probably been through. She was anxious to find out more.

Gabe took Martha's hand and they walked down the hall.

Layke removed his hat and ran his fingers through his hair. "Any updates, Corporal?"

Her breath hitched at the sight of the wavy dark-haired constable. She chastised herself for staring even remotely at the handsome man.

Remember your condition.

After the recent complications from her annual physical, her doctor diagnosed her with polycystic ovary syndrome and said her chances of bearing children were remote. She couldn't give a husband a child. Additionally, her trust in men had wavered ever since she'd discovered her college boyfriend, Colt Fredericks, was the serial rapist targeting women in her campus. Even after all these years, her nightmares from his attack proved she needed to guard her heart. Those nights she'd read her Bible until dawn trying to curb the monsters rolling through her brain. Her favorite passage in Psalms spoke about hovering under God's wings. A place she'd spent many hours.

But the news from her doctor had shattered her world... once again.

Could she trust in His wings when she felt betrayed?

When she no longer knew her purpose in life? *God, help me past this. Show me who I am in You.*

"No new developments on the dark web. Martha has been monitoring it," Corporal Bakker said, interrupting her thoughts. "Call me Elias, please."

"Will do." Layke pulled his notebook from a pocket. "Shall we find out some information from Gabe?"

Hannah bit her lip. "Elias, is it okay if Layke and I talk to the boy alone? He's very nervous and we haven't built his trust yet. I think too many people will scare him."

"Understood. I'll be in my office if you need me. Send my wife back. I need her to work on our books." He disappeared into a room to the right.

Moments later, Layke and Hannah took their coats off in the heated lunchroom. Hannah sat beside Gabe on the couch.

The boy stuffed another Twizzler in his mouth.

Layke sat in a chair opposite them. "Slow down, sport. We'll get you a real supper after we talk. Can you tell us why you were wandering in the woods without a coat? Where did you come from?"

The boy dropped his treat as a tremor shook his limbs.

Hannah pulled the blanket from the back of the couch and wrapped it around him. "It's okay, Gabe. You're safe. You can tell us what happened."

Should they press him right now? Maybe he needed more rest.

"Layke, perhaps we should do this tomorrow after he's had a good night sleep." She needed to protect the boy.

The constable pursed his lips before taking her arm, tugging her off the couch. "We need to get to the bottom of this ring. They have Noel." Layke's whispered words spoke urgency.

"But Gabe is scared."

"I know, but he's safe here."

"He doesn't trust us yet," Hannah said.

Layke positioned his fists on his hips. "We need—"

"I'm okay now." Gabe had come up behind them.

Hannah's heart skipped a beat. The boy made her go to mush. She bent down and hugged him. "You're so brave, Gabe. Are you sure?" She pulled back.

He nodded as his brown eyes filled with tears. "I want to help the other boys."

Hannah stood and glanced at Layke, catching his gaze. Had he heard it, too?

Boys? Did that mean the gang didn't want girls in their operation?

Layke lifted Gabe up and put him back on the couch. "There were no girls there?"

He shook his head.

"Do you know why?" Hannah sat beside him.

He shrugged.

Layke squatted in front of him. "Gabe, tell us what you know."

Gabe's eyes widened. "The bad men will kill the boys at the ranch."

A chill skittered across Hannah's arms despite the warmth in the room.

They needed to find these boys…and fast.

Layke blinked, his breath catching. Had he heard right? He had to find Noel. Now. Maybe Gabe exaggerated. Boys tended to do that, didn't they? Layke examined the look on Gabe's face. The eight-year-old's expression told him he believed what he said. If that was the case, Layke had to locate the rest of the children and stop this gang before more were abducted. To do that, he needed information.

He squeezed Gabe's arm. "It's gonna be okay. We will protect the others. Can you tell us how the bad men took you?"

"Me and my friends were at a campout."

"Wait," Layke said. "In the winter?"

Hannah tilted her head. "Happens all the time here. You can stay warm when you know what you're doing."

"In the snow?"

"Yes, it acts as insulation if you do it correctly."

Something he may have learned as a child if his mother had let him join a boy's club. However, she refused to let him have friends and made him stay outside in the cold for hours on end so she could have her boyfriends over. It was then his disdain for winter had erupted. However, he had learned by the age of six not to argue with his mother or she'd teach him a lesson by beating him. Her blows still haunted him today. Why was he thinking so much about his mother lately? He shrugged off his childhood thoughts and focused on Gabe. "How many of your friends went?"

"Three."

"Your parents were okay with that?"

Gabe averted his gaze but not before Layke caught the sadness in his wet eyes. This boy had a story to tell.

"I don't have a mommy or daddy. I live at the Frontier Group Home."

Hannah sighed as her shoulders slumped. She fiddled with the bag of licorice.

It was clear to Layke she'd grown attached to this boy. Already. Or was it something else that had her agitated? "Were your buddies from there, too?"

"Yes," Gabe said.

Hannah grabbed his hand. "How long have you lived there?"

"Not sure. Sister Daphne told me I was left on the doorstep of a different group home when I was a baby. They moved me to Frontier after no one wanted me."

She winced and stared at her hands, twiddling the ring

on her right finger. "Do you know anything about your parents?"

Layke noted Hannah's reaction to the news of Gabe being an orphan. What had caused that subtle change in her demeanor?

"They didn't love me enough to keep me," the boy said.

Layke wrote the group home's and Sister Daphne's names down. He would call her later for more details. Again, his own past lurked in the background. Different than Gabe's, but there were times he had wished to be somewhere other than with his mother. Had she ever loved him? She couldn't have, with all the lies she told.

"That can't be true, Gabe," Hannah said. "I also lived at a group home when I was younger. One day you will be adopted like me."

The boy's eyes brightened. "You were? Did your new family love you?"

Hannah stared at the floor.

She was stalling. Why?

She looked up and cupped Gabe's chin with her hand. "After we got used to living together, they did. Your new family will love you very much."

His lip quivered.

"I promise." She rubbed his cheek. "Tell us about the other boys."

Smart girl. Divert his attention to something else.

"They're my best buds in the whole wide world. We do everything together. Fish, skip rocks, build forts."

Finally, children who weren't glued to their computers. He respected kids who played outside and used their imaginations.

Layke swallowed the thickening in his throat. Gabe's story had affected him more than he'd realized. "How many were at the campout?"

"All my buds, plus other boys."

"From the group home?" Hannah asked.

"No. I didn't know them."

Layke wrote a note. "Tell us what happened."

"We were singing songs in front of the fire, making s'mores. Then three men circled us. They pointed guns at the leaders from our home and told them not to move or they'd shoot." He stopped.

Layke squeezed his shoulder. "It's okay. They can't get you here. What did they do?"

Gabe bit into another Twizzler before continuing. "They grabbed some of us and said we were coming with them. Our leader jumped up to stop them, and one man hit him in the head with his gun." Big tears spilled down his cheeks and he sniffed.

Hannah gasped and pulled the boy into her arms. "That must have been scary for you to see. I'm so sorry." She turned to Layke. "We need to give him a break."

He bit the inside of his cheek. Her mothering slowed them down. He needed answers. A thought crossed his mind and he jumped up. "I have to make a call. Let's take five minutes."

Layke stepped into the hall and punched a number into his cell phone.

"Hi, Layke. Do you have news?" His half brother's weakened voice revealed his worry.

"I might have a lead, and need to ask you a question, Murray."

"Shoot."

"When you said Noel was kidnapped from a winter retreat, was it only for boys?"

"Yes, boys from our church."

Same MO as Gabe. Boys taken from a winter camping trip. They targeted them when they were away from their homes. Why? Easy access? Same gang? "Do you know how many were taken?"

"Four."

"Can you text me the parents' names and numbers?"

"Will do. Layke, find my boy."

"I will. I promise." How could he say that? He'd just broken a rule he always held. *Never promise anything to a victim's family.*

"Layke, Noel is autistic and doesn't do well when he's out of his comfort zone."

Wait—what? He slumped against the wall. "Why didn't you tell me this before?"

"I thought I had."

"No. Don't autistic children have challenges with social interaction? Why did you send him on a retreat?"

A sigh sounded on the other end of the call. "I wanted to try and help him make friends. Natalie didn't want to send him, but I insisted." His voice quivered. "It's all my fault."

Layke clamped his eyes shut as he pictured Murray's pain. He had to help his half brother. He opened his eyes and straightened his posture. "I will do everything in my power to find him fast."

Another promise.

Stop breaking your rules, Layke.

He said his goodbyes and told Murray he'd keep him up to speed. As much as he could, of course. He walked back into the lunchroom and stopped short.

Hannah rocked Gabe as she sang to him. A red curl escaped from her ponytail and bounced forward. Her love of children was evident.

He cleared his throat and stepped forward. "We need to continue."

She stopped singing and narrowed her eyes.

Obviously he had irritated her, but he pushed it from his mind. "Sorry. We need to find out more answers."

She pursed her lips yet nodded.

Layke's cell phone dinged, announcing a text. Murray

had sent him a list of names and phone numbers. Good. He'd contact them later. He shoved his phone in his pocket and sat. "Sport, can you tell me what happened next?"

"The bad men made us get in their vans."

"Can you tell me where they took you?"

Gabe shook his head. "They covered our eyes."

Of course. They wouldn't want the boys knowing their secret location. "How long of a drive was it?"

He shrugged.

Layke was afraid of that. Gabe was too young to remember details. "Can you tell us anything about the drive there?"

His eyes lit up. "Yes! It was bumpy. You know, like this." He bounced and rocked in his seat.

Yukon probably had many side roads. Not helpful. "What did you see after you got there?"

"A cave."

Now they were getting somewhere, but why would they take them there? Layke scratched his head. "Can you describe it?"

"We had to duck to get inside and the bad men couldn't come in without crawling."

"Could they stand once they were in the cave?"

"No. They're too tall."

Layke eyed Hannah. Her expression twisted.

Could that be why they had chosen children to do the work?

"What did you do inside?" Hannah asked.

"They wanted us to dig."

Hannah flexed her hands and curled her lips.

Her body language revealed clearly the anger churning inside.

Layke suppressed the urge to throw something and turned back to the boy. "Dig what?"

Gabe bit his lip and looked away. "I don't know."

He's hiding something but what? "You can tell us, Gabe."

"I told you. I don't know." His voice quivered.

Interesting. He'd try a different tactic. "Can you tell us what the men look like?"

"They had dark masks on."

"They never took them off?"

Gabe leaned forward. "I remember. One did when he took a drink."

Layke stood and circled the small lunchroom. "Can you describe him?"

The boy scrunched his face.

Hannah smiled. "Did the man have dark or light skin?"

"Light."

"Okay, what about the color of his hair?"

She knew how to translate his questions. Good. He never had been good around children. They made him nervous.

Gabe contorted his face. "It was spiky."

Hannah stiffened and glanced at Layke.

What about that description had her on edge? He moved back to the chair and sat. He'd ask her about it later. He needed to request Corporal Bakker to get a forensic artist here to draw a sketch. The vague description would at least give them a start.

Gabe yawned.

"Layke, we need to get him—"

Pop! Pop! Pop!

Layke bolted out of his chair and unleashed his weapon. "Get down!"

Hannah pulled Gabe off the couch onto the floor and threw her body over his, shielding him.

Screams filled the corridor.

The detachment was under attack.

FOUR

Hannah wrapped her arms around Gabe's shaking body. His whimpers tore her apart. This boy had wormed his way into her heart…already. She vowed to do anything to protect him from these unknown assailants even if it meant putting a target on her back. She didn't care. He was worth the danger. Their pasts were too much alike for her to ignore this sweet boy. Memories of the group home she had lived in, foster care families and bullies slammed her back to her unstable childhood. A place she had locked into the recesses of her mind and thrown away the key. With Gabe's news, it threatened to spill out, but she didn't have time to deal with prior hurts. Besides, in the end her story had turned out okay even if she had to go through many valleys to reach her mountaintop family.

"Shh…it's okay. We've got you." Hannah uttered a silent prayer asking God to watch over them.

"They found me." Gabe's lip quivered.

Layke raised his gun and turned the doorknob. "I'm going to check it out. Stay here. Lock the door. Only open it for me. You hear?"

"Yes."

He eased his way out the door.

Hannah jumped up and turned the lock. *Lord, help the enemy not to find us here.* She pressed her ear to the door to see if she could hear anything. A crash sounded in the distance. Were they getting closer? Was it the man with the spiked hair again? She pulled out her Beretta and held it at her side. She wouldn't be caught unaware. Gabe had to be protected.

Footsteps thudded outside in the hall. The knob twisted but the lock held. Someone shook the handle.

Hannah gasped and jumped to the right of the door and put her finger to her lips, indicating for Gabe to be quiet. Her heart ricocheted. She willed it to be silent for fear of being heard.

"We know you're here somewhere, Hannah Morgan," the voice boomed. "You might as well come out and bring the boy. He's ours."

How did they know her name and where to find them?

Gabe whimpered beside the couch.

She rushed over to him and pulled him back into her arms. "Shh," she whispered.

"You'll pay a high price if you don't give in to our demands," the man shouted. "We know all about you. You can't hide."

What?

Gunfire erupted somewhere in the detachment.

A tremor slunk down Hannah's neck and threatened to engulf her entire body. Was Layke okay?

Please, Lord. Bring him back to us safely.

Another crash was followed by rushing footsteps. Close. Closer. She held her breath and raised her weapon toward the door.

The wall's clock ticked, reminding her of precious time.

Someone rapped on the door.

"Hannah, it's me. Open up."

Layke.

She jumped up, turned the lock and yanked open the door. He rushed in and closed it. "We need to go."

"How? I heard the gunfire. They're too close. He could get hurt."

"I created a diversion with the other constables and Elias. The culprits are headed in another direction. We're going out the back. I found this oversize coat in a locker." He wrapped the parka around Gabe and picked him up. "We're gonna get you to safety, sport."

Hannah grabbed her coat and threw it on, pushing away the fear. Her adrenaline kicked in and she gripped her weapon tighter. "Ready."

"We need to stay really quiet, Gabe. Can you do that?"

The boy nodded and latched on to Layke's neck.

"Hang on and don't let go." Layke turned to her. "Follow me and watch for anyone sneaking up behind us."

"Got it." She eased the door open and looked both ways. "Clear."

Layke held Gabe with one arm and lifted his weapon with the other, stepping out into the hall. He headed left toward the rear of the detachment.

She followed, raised her gun and turned constantly to ensure they weren't being chased.

Shots were fired in the opposite direction. Good, Layke's diversion worked.

Within seconds, they had reached the back door.

Layke peered out. "I don't see anyone, but they could be lurking in the shadows. We're going to make a run for it." He holstered his weapon and pulled out a key fob. "Got these from Mrs. Bakker. We're taking Constable Antoine's Suburban since it's parked out back. I need you to cover me. Have you been trained in defensive tactics?"

She gritted her teeth. Did he not think her capable of giving protection?

"Of course." Her curt tone surprised even herself, but she was tired of having to prove her abilities. Still, she'd never come across this type of lethal assailant in her five-year stint with the CBSA. She'd seen a lot on the job but hadn't had to protect a boy from something this powerful. *You can do this.* Did she doubt herself?

"Sorry, didn't mean to imply anything. Let's go." He pushed the door open and stepped outside. "Hurry." He rushed toward the vehicle.

Hannah raised her weapon and followed him into the subzero temperatures. The wind bit her face and she winced but ignored it, keeping her focus on the task of protecting the two males suddenly thrust into her life. She ran after him as she pointed her 9 mm in different directions and looked for gunmen. Beams from the lone streetlight bounced on the fresh-fallen snow as more fell around them. The dim lighting made it difficult for her to locate any assailants, but so far they appeared to be in the clear.

Layke placed Gabe in the back seat. "Buckle him in." He opened the driver's door and jumped in, starting the vehicle.

She holstered her weapon, climbed in beside the boy and fastened his seat belt.

Layke pulled the Suburban out of the parking lot without the lights on and took a back road.

"Do you know where you're going?" she asked.

"Nope, just didn't want to go out the front."

Good point.

An idea popped into her mind. "A friend of mine has a cabin in the woods about thirty miles from here. We could hide there."

"We can't put her in danger."

"She's not there. She left yesterday for a trip to Hawaii."

Layke hesitated.

She could almost tell what he was thinking. "I know where the key is. She told me I was welcome to go there if I ever needed to get away. I think this qualifies, don't you?"

"Definitely." He peered in the rearview mirror. "Looks

like we got away undetected. That will make them angry and they won't give up. Which direction do we take?"

She guided him through the streets to get them out of the small town toward the cabin.

Moments later, he pulled onto the AlCan Highway. Thankfully, the road was somewhat deserted. Most residents had probably made their way home from work and were settled in from the winter elements. Too bad *they* weren't.

The snow intensified and the vehicle fishtailed, swerving toward the ditch.

"Hang on!" Layke yelled.

Gabe screamed.

She pulled him closer as if that would protect him from the dangerous icy highway.

If it wasn't gunmen out to get them, it was Mother Nature.

They couldn't catch a break.

Layke righted the vehicle back onto the road as two headlights blocked their path like a speeding train.

The car headed directly toward them, locked in an icy skid.

Layke ignored Gabe's scream and jerked the wheel left, catching the tire in a rut of ice and snow deposited by a snowplow. The Suburban lurched back toward the oncoming car.

Hannah gasped.

The car inched closer as if time passed in slow motion. Layke held his breath waiting for impact.

At the last moment, the driver lay on the horn and swerved around them.

Layke let out a swoosh of air. He pulled them back onto the right side of the highway.

"Good driving, Constable," Hannah said.

"Thanks." He'd had lots of practice on the deadly winter roads along the Banff Highway near his home in Calgary.

"God kept us safe."

He glanced over his shoulder at her. Did she really believe that?

"What? You don't believe in God?" she asked.

Did his face reveal how he felt about someone he couldn't see or touch? The same someone who hadn't intervened whenever he'd supposedly disobeyed his mother and faced the wrath of her fist? He turned his eyes back to the snowy road. No, he wouldn't let God in his life. Now or ever.

"I don't." He'd leave it at that.

"Why?"

"God loves you, Mr. Layke." Gabe's soft voice boomed in his ear.

Not him, too. Layke was surrounded.

"That's right, Gabe," Hannah said. "He loves all of us. No matter what."

He needed to change the subject. He wasn't willing to go there. "How much longer to the cabin?"

"About twenty minutes," Hannah replied.

Great. That was an eternity if they wanted to talk about God. He had to steer the conversation in a different direction. "Sport, what do you want to be when you grow up?"

"A brave policeman like you."

Layke gulped and pushed the unexpected emotions away. This boy knew how to capture his hardened heart. When had Layke become so closed?

You know when.

A memory surfaced.

Mommy, why can't I go with the other boys to the park? His six-year-old mind hadn't been able to comprehend why his mom hated him so much.

Her hazel eyes had narrowed, flashing like a flame spitting in a bonfire. *Little boy, you will do as your mother says.*

But all the other kids get to go. Why not me?

She'd rushed over and slapped him across the face. Hard.

His hand had flown to his stinging cheek as he toppled backward over the chair. Tears followed and his breath came in raspy spurts.

Don't be a baby. You are such a spoiled little—

A blaring horn wrenched him back to the present.

"Watch out, Layke!"

He pulled the vehicle back into the right lane. *Stupid!*

The memory of the first time she had hit him had caused his concentration to waver. He couldn't let that happen again. His mother had brought enough pain into his life. He didn't need to add to it by having an accident.

"How much longer?" he asked.

"Almost at the turnoff—it's hard to see in this snowstorm."

She wasn't wrong. The snow would not let up. He turned the wipers to full speed and still had problems seeing through the fat white flakes plaguing them. He rubbed at the condensation forming on the inside of the windshield. Great, as if his view wasn't already blocked enough. He bit his lip to stop him from uttering a word he'd later regret, especially in front of the boy.

"There!" Hannah leaned in between the seats and pointed left. "That's the road to take."

He flipped on the signal and pulled on to the snowy road. "How far? This road is not in good condition." He swerved to miss a mound of snow.

"Five minutes."

"I'm hungry," Gabe said.

The boy's whine matched Layke's frame of mind.

"I hear ya, sport. Me, too." He glanced over his shoulder. "I hope there's food at this cabin."

"Should be. It's winterized, as she comes out here most weekends, so I'm sure we'll find something."

The deserted road wove around a bend. Layke held the wheel tight to keep the vehicle steady. The only light came from the Suburban. Not a soul in sight.

Good. They could hide.

Ten minutes later Hannah pointed again. "That's it."

A driveway sat off to the right. He turned up the incline, plowing through the white mess. He held his breath and willed the tires to keep moving. They couldn't get stuck now.

Snow-covered spruce branches drooped low from the intense weight and created a winter wonderland path to the cabin in the woods. The tires spun but quickly gained traction. The small timber structure came into view. A veranda wrapped around the cabin, trees swallowing it on all sides as if sentinels protecting its occupants.

He only hoped that was true.

Layke pulled in front and shut off the engine. "Safe and sound."

"Thank the good Lord," Hannah said.

Not again. If He was good, He would never have allowed these children to be taken in the first place. He opened his door. "Let's get inside out of this wretched weather."

They climbed from the vehicle and up the stairs.

Hannah moved a heavy flowerpot and produced a key. "Told you."

He crossed his arms. "Isn't that a little too much of a cliché? This isn't TV."

She shrugged and opened the front door.

They stomped the snow from their boots and moved farther inside.

Hannah removed her footwear and headed toward a hall. "I'll turn on the propane tank to get the heat going. You start the fire. It's in the living room."

Layke helped Gabe take off his boots and did the same. "Keep your coat on for now." He stepped through the wooden archway into a hunter's oasis.

A brick fireplace sat in the center of the far wall. Timber beams lined the ceiling with plank wood walls on all sides, creating a rustic feel. Two plush chairs with an end table in between sat in the middle of a large window. A wooden-legged coffee table with a glass top rested in the center on top of a multicolored woven Aztec rug.

"So cool!" Gabe came up behind him.

"Indeed it is, sport."

Layke eyed the wood piled next to the hearth. Odd they'd have propane as well as a wood-burning fireplace. He opened the screen and placed kindling on the iron rack. After finding matches on the mantel, he struck one and lit the wood.

"Did you learn that in Scouts?" Gabe asked.

He pursed his lips. "No, I taught myself."

"That's what we were learning before the bad men came."

Layke caught the fear in Gabe's clouded eyes. He squeezed his shoulder. "You're safe here."

"You promise?"

Layke sighed inwardly. "Yes."

Another promise he'd probably regret.

The kindling caught and a spark spit upward. Layke placed a small log on top.

Gabe knelt in front of the fire and held out his hands. "Can we roast marshmallows?"

Layke tousled the boy's curls. "We'll see if there's any in the kitchen."

"What's in the kitchen?" Hannah eyed his fire. "Nice. I can feel the heat already."

Gabe jumped up and hugged her legs. "We're gonna roast marshmallows!"

Hannah raised her brow at Layke.

"If we have any," he said.

"I'll go see what I can find to eat." Hannah walked into the kitchen and rustled around. She returned within minutes holding a can of beans and had something hidden behind her back. "Beans okay? They're maple flavored."

Gabe turned up his nose.

Layke did the same. "I guess we don't have much of a choice."

Hannah's blue eyes twinkled in the light. She had also let her hair down. It fell around her shoulders in soft red curls.

He couldn't help but stare at her intoxicating beauty.

She waved something in front of his face. "Earth to Layke."

Caught in the act.

He cleared his throat as Gabe giggled.

"Look what I have?" She pulled a bag of marshmallows out from behind her back.

Gabe jumped up and squealed. "Yay!"

"Looks like you'll get your wish, Gabe."

"I'll go start supper and then later we can roast these." Hannah smiled at Layke and walked back into the kitchen.

He stood. "I gotta make some calls. You stay here."

He roamed down the hall in search of a room to call the names Murray had sent him earlier. Hopefully they had some information that would help.

Fifteen minutes later, he'd spoken to all but one and he'd left a message for the father to call him back. Unfortunately, the other parents didn't know anything and only pleaded with him to find their sons. Alive.

He plunked himself on the bed and rubbed his chest, the weight of the case sitting heavy with the pressure to bring it to a close.

He needed to talk to Corporal Bakker again, so he keyed in the man's number.

"Bakker here."

"It's Layke. Can you get a forensic artist to Beaver Creek? We need to see if we can get a composite of the man Gabe saw."

"I'll send in a request right now, but the nearest one is five hours away in Whitehorse. Where are you?"

"In a cabin thirty minutes north of Beaver Creek. It belongs to a friend of Officer Morgan's. Can you let the other constables know our whereabouts but no one else? The less who know, the better."

"Agreed. You need to keep the boy safe. He's our only source of information on this gang right now." He paused. "Listen, Constable Yellowhead said he couldn't track down the snowmobile. He followed the tracks, but they ended abruptly. We think they drove onto a truck to escape."

Layke flattened his lips. "Not surprised."

"Oh, and one of the assailants at the detachment attack who escaped was injured. We're checking nearby hospitals and clinics."

The wind howled and shook the cabin.

"Okay, I'll—"

A crash sounded from the living room.

Gabe screamed.

FIVE

Hannah threw the pot of beans onto the propane stove, slopping them over the side, and ran into the living room. Gabe sat crying on the floor in front of a fallen broken lamp. She knelt beside him.

"What's wrong?" She pulled him into her arms.

Layke stumbled into the room, his eyes wild. "What happened?"

"I was looking out the window and I saw a face staring at me. I knocked over the lamp. I'm sorry." He sniffed and wiped his nose on his sleeve.

"No worries, Gabe. You're okay." She glanced at Layke and gestured toward outside.

He nodded and pulled out his Maglite. "I'll go check around the cabin." He put on his coat and boots and opened the door.

The brisk wind slithered into the room like a snake stalking its prey. Hannah grabbed one of the Aztec throws and wrapped it around Gabe. "Layke will check it out. It was probably the shadow of an animal. There are coyotes in these parts."

He stiffened. "There are?"

Oops. Not a good idea to share that information. "I'm sure they're long gone now." She poked him in the belly. "Your scream probably scared them."

He giggled. "Maybe."

"How about you help me set the table for supper?"

He jumped up, discarding the blanket. "Yes. I want marshmallows for dessert."

She stood and crossed her arms. "We'll see. It's almost bedtime for you."

"Aw… I can stay up a little later. Maybe just one?" His widened eyes blinked as if pleading with her.

She sighed. This boy knew how to get her to cave. "Okay."

He jumped up and down. "Yay!"

She ushered him into the kitchen, giving him a little nudge. "Time to set the table." She pulled plates from the cupboard and handed them to him. "Now, be careful."

Hannah watched him over her shoulder as he made sure each place setting was exactly the same distance apart. *Too cute.* Why hadn't anyone adopted this adorable boy? Images flashed through her mind as she pictured the first time she had walked into the kitchen of her new family's home. Her new brother had sat at the table with his arms crossed, clearly displaying his disdain for having a baby sister he'd never wanted. Their relationship had been rocky at first, along with her mother's, but over time and trials they'd become the family they were today. One who stood beside one another. *Why couldn't Gabe have one, too, Lord?*

The door burst open, slamming against the wall from the wind's force and bringing her back into the moment.

She jumped and almost dropped a glass.

Layke shook off the snow from his coat and removed his boots. "We're all clear. I only saw animal tracks."

"Good." Hannah turned on the gas burner to warm up the beans. "Supper will be ready in five minutes." She rummaged through the pantry for something to go with their meal and only found crackers.

Moments later, they sat around the table as she served

the beans. "Now, how's this for a gourmet meal? Chez Hannah's is the spot to be tonight, huh?"

Gabe started to fill his spoon, but Hannah stopped him. "How about we say grace first?" She held out both her hands. One to Gabe and the other to Layke.

"I forgot." Gabe took her left.

Although Layke's contorted face revealed his annoyance at the thought of praying, she tilted her head to silently plead with him while wiggling the fingers of her right hand.

He sighed and took it, bowing his head.

Lord, work on his heart. "Father, thank You for keeping us safe. Be with us tonight. Give us a nice evening and a good sleep. Bless this food to our body's use. In Jesus' name, Amen."

"Amen!" Gabe grabbed his spoon, filled it with beans and shoved it into his mouth.

Layke smiled and took a sip of water. "Sport, take your time."

"But I'm hungry," he mumbled in between bites.

Poor guy. He'd probably gone most of the day without food. The thought sparked a question in her mind. "Gabe, you mentioned you had to dig in a cave. Did you sleep there, too?"

She bit her lip as she waited for an answer, hoping the abductors had, at least, fed them and provided shelter. However, she'd heard horror stories in other smuggling cases.

"We slept at the ranch." He took another rounded spoonful.

Hannah glanced at Layke.

He stopped eating. "Gabe, where is this ranch? Do you know?"

The boy paused and shook his head.

"They blindfolded you, didn't they?" They had when

transporting them to the cave, so why not follow the same pattern when taking them to the ranch? At least they had the decency to give them a proper roof over their heads.

"Yes."

Hannah smothered a gasp as a horrible thought entered her mind. "Were they nice to you? Treat you okay?"

"The lady at the ranch made yummy suppers and packed us lunches."

A woman? Hannah couldn't imagine a woman allowing men to kidnap children and keep them hostage. What kind of person would knowingly help a ruthless gang? Obviously, not someone who was a mother or wanted to be one. She placed her hand on her abdomen. What she wouldn't do to be able to feel a child growing inside her. Of course, she wasn't in a relationship anyway and struggled with the thought of never giving a husband a child. *God, why did You allow my dreams to be crushed?* Tears threatened to form and she looked down, though not before catching Layke's eye. He'd been watching her. Great. Now he'd interrogate her. She rose from the table and rushed to the sink, setting her dish there. Anything to avoid those piercing blue eyes.

"Can you describe the woman?" Layke asked.

Hannah glanced back at the table.

Layke's attention now focused on Gabe. Good.

"She has yellow hair, glasses, and is…you know…" He sucked in his belly.

Hannah stifled a giggle.

"You mean she had a really small tummy?" The corner of Layke's mouth turned upward. Seemed he was also trying hard not to laugh.

"Yes. Skinny." He took a bite and swallowed. "But she was nice."

"So, when the men brought you to the ranch, did they take their masks off?" Hannah sat back down at the table.

"No. They didn't stay."

"They dropped you off and left?" Layke took a spoonful of beans.

"Yup. The other men with big guns made sure we didn't leave. They locked us in our rooms after supper."

"Did you see their faces?"

"No, they also wore masks."

Hannah sat and touched his arm. "Do you remember anything else?"

He scrunched his lips together. "Nope."

His body language screamed evasion. There was something he was hiding or was he protecting someone?

If so, why?

Layke studied the boy. Gabe's eyes darted back and forth as if searching for a spot to land his gaze. His hands fumbled with his utensils. Clearly something had him rattled, but what? He held back information. How could Layke get the boy to talk?

He reached over and covered his large hand over Gabe's small one. "Sport, you can trust us. We won't let them hurt you ever again."

Gabe pulled his hand out from under Layke's. "But can you get my friends out?"

Layke leaned back in his chair. Could he if they didn't even know where they were? He had also promised Murray he'd get Noel back. His jaw tightened. He needed to stop promising things he couldn't guarantee. However, he could promise one thing. "Gabe, I will do whatever I can to find them, but you have to help us. Do you remember anything that could lead us to the ranch where you were being held?"

Gabe crossed his hands and let out a heavy sigh. He pressed his lips shut.

Layke moved his chair closer to the boy's and draped his arm across Gabe's back. "Any small detail will help."

Gabe wiggled away from him and jumped up. "I can't!" He ran into the living room.

Hannah slouched farther into her chair. "You have to stop pressuring him. He's still frightened."

"What's going on with you? You know my nephew is also missing. I need to find him, and Gabe is holding something back."

She stood. "Nothing is going on and I understand your urgency to find Noel, but pressing Gabe isn't going to help. He needs to fully trust us."

Layke's cell phone rang. He stood and pulled it out. "I need to take this. Excuse me." He walked down the hall and stepped inside a bedroom. He had tried to hold back his frustration with Hannah, but she was becoming too attached to the boy. It clouded her judgment. He pressed Answer on his phone. "Jackson here."

"Layke buddy. How are you?"

Layke smiled.

His best bud, Hudson Steeves, always brought a smile to his face. They had met working at a homeless shelter in Windsor, Ontario, and became fast friends—even went to police college together. Layke checked his watch. "Hey, so good to hear your voice. You just finishing shift?"

"No. Did some running around tonight with Kaylin for wedding preparations. Heading home now."

Hudson's fiancée, CBSA officer Kaylin Poirier, had recently helped him crack a major drug smuggling ring. They were now engaged and planning their wedding. Interesting how their relationship had started with them being thrust together in a joint task force operation.

There was no way he would start a relationship with someone he worked with. His crush on a fellow officer who'd tried to sabotage his reputation had left him with a bad taste in his mouth when it came to romance. He'd experienced the hurt firsthand. The phrase—*been there, done that, not doing it again*—raced through his mind. Plus, he'd promised himself he would never have kids. Not after the pain and suffering he'd gone through in his childhood.

He shook off the thought and concentrated on the conversation. "Have you decided on a date yet?"

"That's why I'm calling. We have. October third and I have a question for you. Will you be my best man?"

"I'd be honored." At least one of them was happy.

"Sweet. I heard about your case. I'm praying for your protection."

Right. His bud was a Christian. He was surrounded. "Not sure that will help."

"Layke, when will you believe?"

He raked a hand through his hair. "Now's not a good time to talk about God to me, Hudson."

His friend sighed. "Sorry. I know your mother left a huge hole in your heart. You need to forgive."

Layke clasped his eyes shut and resisted the urge to throw the phone across the room. He needed to get out of this funk. But how?

Trust.

Why did that word come to his mind so easily when it was something he found hard to do?

"I appreciate your prayers. I do. I'm just not ready."

"You also know that Amber's death wasn't your fault, right?"

More images of his previous partner's body threatened to overtake him. Another reason he could never let a woman into his life again. He'd paid the price dearly with Amber Maurier's betrayal. The question remained—why couldn't he get past it? "Listen, I gotta run. I'm happy for you and can't wait for your big day." Would happiness ever be in Layke's future?

"Chat later, bud. Miss you." He clicked off.

Layke shoved his cell phone back into his pocket.

"Mr. Layke, marshmallow time!" Gabe yelled from the living room.

Layke snickered. At least this boy knew how to lighten his mood. He opened the door and made his way to the living room.

And stopped in his tracks.

Hannah had changed into lounging pants and a plaid shirt. She was breathtaking.

"What?" Hannah asked.

Oops. She'd caught him staring. He cleared his throat. "Your friend's clothes?"

"Yes, thankfully we're the same size. She's married and her hubby's clothes may fit you. I put some on the bed of the far bedroom."

"Thanks." He walked over and sat by the fire.

Gabe stuffed a marshmallow on a long wire. "Time to roast marshmallows."

"Where did you get that?" Layke pointed to the metal stick.

"Miss Hannah made it out of a hanger."

Inventive. "Where did you learn that?"

She pulled an inhaler out of her pocket and took a shot of the medicine. "Seriously? You never roasted marshmallows as a kid?" She took the hanger from Gabe's hand and sat in front of the fire. "Let me do it."

"I'm afraid not. My mother would never—" He stopped. He wasn't ready to share his past.

She looked up. "Never what?"

"Nothing." Only Hudson knew about his mother and he wanted to keep it that way. "Show me how it's done." He knelt beside them.

She stuck the marshmallow over the coals, turning it over and over.

Layke draped his arm around Gabe's shoulders and peered at Hannah. It was like a family gathering. He could almost get used to this.

Almost.

Hannah finished roasting and held the marshmallow over to Gabe. "It's hot. Be careful." She eyed Layke. His relaxed shoulders told her the constable had given up whatever war he battled for this special moment here at the cabin. How long would it last? Something from his past held him in a tight grip. Would he ever share it with her?

She breathed in the smell of crackling wood. One of her favorite scents. She could get used to this. A handsome man and a sweet boy at her side.

And then she remembered.

It would never happen for her. No husband or child would call her blessed like she'd read in the Bible. *Why, Lord?* Doubts of her identity in Christ threatened to encompass her again as thoughts of motherhood were stolen from her future. Why did she associate her status with whether or not she could have children? Didn't God love her for who she was?

She quenched a sigh. She'd deal with that hurt later. "You're next, Layke." She grabbed another marshmallow.

He raised his hands in a stop position. "No, no. I don't need one."

"Oh, yes, you do." She stuck it over the coals.

He grinned as the fire reflection danced in his beautiful blue eyes.

Her heartbeat quickened and her throat clogged. *Stop thinking of Layke in that way, Hannah.*

Not only was he off-limits, but he also lived in Calgary. She would not do long-distance.

Besides, he probably had a girlfriend.

Plus, it was said that relationships formed under intense circumstances never last. She wouldn't be another statistic.

Once the marshmallow appeared golden, she held it over to Layke. "Here you go. It's hot."

He touched it and snapped his hand back. "Ouch!"

"Told you." She giggled. "Gabe, it's time—"

A snore interrupted her sentence. She glanced over at the boy. He'd curled up on the floor with the blanket and had fallen asleep.

Layke followed her gaze. "He's had a rough day. Time for bed." He lifted Gabe and held him over his shoulder, blanket and all. "Which bedroom?"

Did he know how adorable he looked with the boy?

Stop, Hannah. She stood. "Follow me."

She led him down the hall and opened the middle room's door in the three-bedroom cabin. Her friend was a doctor, so this amazing cabin gave her an oasis away from a hectic schedule. This room was decorated in a nautical theme. A single bed, adorned with a white comforter and blue-striped pillow, sat in the middle of the room. The headboard contained a shelf holding a buoy and sailboat. The nightstands held matching lighthouse lamps. The white-and-navy-striped walls added to the ambiance.

"Wow. This is every sailor's dream room. Nice." Layke's soft voice broke the silence.

"I know, right? Wait till you see your room at the end of the hall."

His forehead crinkled.

"I'll let you discover it for yourself." She removed the throw pillows from the bed and tugged the comforters back.

Layke tucked Gabe under the covers and pulled them tight to his small body.

They tiptoed out of the room and Hannah closed the

door. "How about you change and then we can talk about the case?"

"Sounds good." He headed down the hall.

Hannah walked back into the living room, stoked the fire with the poker and added a log. Even though they had turned on the cabin's heat, the room still held a chill to it. She closed the screen and went to the window to check the storm.

She pulled the drapes and peered out but could only see darkness. She turned on the porch light to check the surroundings. Snow fell hard as the wind whipped around the fir trees. A branch close to the cabin slammed against the window.

She gasped and jumped back.

Calm down, Hannah. You're safe here.

At least she prayed they were.

Her cell phone buzzed and she grabbed it from her lounge pants pocket. She peered at the name. Her boss.

"Doyle. Good to hear from you." Outside of work hours, she always referred to her superintendent as Doyle. He'd helped her through many trying times over the years as she trained with all men. He was the only one who understood how it felt to be an outcast. His sister had been bullied as a child and he'd tried to protect her, which alienated him from the other kids at school.

"You sound chipper. You're safe?"

"Yes. For now anyway."

"Where are you?"

"You remember my friend Taryn?"

"The doctor?"

"Yes. She and her hubby have a cabin thirty minutes north of Beaver Creek. We're hunkered down here during the storm."

"You and the boy?"

"And Layke."

"Oh…so it's just Layke now? Not Constable?"

His tone revealed the smile he probably had plastered on his face. He'd been trying to set her up with guy after guy for years. "Stop. It's not like that."

"Hannah, you deserve happiness."

She rubbed her belly. No, she couldn't put a man through the pain. "You find out anything about possible child smugglers from other border patrol stations?"

"Nice dodge." He laughed. "I've contacted them all and they are aware of the situation but haven't seen anything suspicious. Yet. I asked them to contact me if they do."

"Good."

"You find out anything from the boy?"

Hannah told him about their interview with Gabe. "He gave a description of one of the masked men and it sounds like the same man I saw at the station."

"No names?"

"Nothing. He's holding back on us though. Seems scared to trust us."

"He will in no time with your charm."

"Funny."

Layke walked into the room wearing jeans and the buffalo plaid flannel shirt she'd found earlier. She sucked in a breath. The tight fit revealed his protruding muscles.

"What's wrong?" Doyle asked.

Oops. She hadn't realized she'd gasped out loud. "Nothing. I gotta run."

"Stay safe and keep me updated."

"Will do." She clicked off. "Hey, that red and black looks good on you." Had she just said that out loud? *Rein it in.*

"Thanks. It's a bit tight but okay."

She bit her tongue to avoid saying something she'd regret. "I was just talking to my boss. He said he didn't get any further info from the other border stations."

He sat on the plush couch and took out his notebook. "I've called in a forensic artist, plus Elias told me one of the assailants was injured in the gunfire at the station. He got away though. Constables are searching nearby hospitals and clinics."

"Good. Let's talk about what we have so far." She sat on the adjacent couch and pulled the Aztec blanket over her.

They spent time going over what they knew. Unfortunately, it wasn't a lot. They needed a break. Who was the man with the spiked hair and where was he hiding?

Two hours later, Hannah flicked on the TV. She needed to unwind and television would do it for her. An episode of *Bones* popped on the screen. "Oh, I love this show." She curled her legs underneath her and gathered the blanket closer, ready to watch her favorite anthropologist. A scene of Brennan and Hodgins being buried alive boomed tension throughout the room.

Layke gasped, stood and grabbed the remote from her hand, turning the station. "I can't watch that." He plunked himself back in his seat.

Hannah uncurled her legs and leaned forward. "What? Why?"

He bit his lip.

An uncharacteristic action for the fierce policeman. Definitely not the Superman image she had of him in the little time she'd gotten to know him. "What's wrong?"

He turned off the TV. "I had an incident in my childhood that sparked a fear of being buried alive."

Her mouth fell open. Not what she expected. "I'm so sorry. I didn't—"

A thud from down the hall was followed by a blood-curdling scream.

"Gabe!"

SIX

Hannah threw off the blanket and bolted from the couch. She raced down the hall with Layke at her heels. *Lord, help Gabe to be okay.* Had they found them? Had they somehow gotten in through the back entrance? She swung the door open. It banged against the wall, the thud resonating throughout the small room. Hannah winced and turned the light on. Gabe rocked in the corner and whimpered with his thumb in his mouth. Not an action for the more mature eight-year-old she'd seen earlier.

Layke entered with his weapon raised.

She gazed around the room and found no one. However, something had scared the boy. She reached over and put her hand on Layke's gun, lowering it. "You'll scare him."

He nodded.

Hannah walked over to the boy and knelt beside him. "What is it, Gabe?"

He pulled his thumb from his mouth. "He. He. Found. Me." The boy's stuttered words made no sense.

"There's no one here, sport." Layke had stuffed his gun in the back of his jeans and joined them on the floor.

"But I saw him."

Layke glanced at Hannah.

The boy must have been hallucinating. Could intense

fear cause that to happen? First, the face in the window and now this?

Layke scooped Gabe into his arms. "Let's get you back into bed."

Gabe squirmed. "He's coming for me."

Layke tucked the covers all around him, creating a cocoon-like effect as if shielding him from an unknown assailant. He sat on the bed.

Hannah plunked herself down on the other side of Gabe and hoped their combined presence would help him feel protected. She rubbed his cheek. "It's okay, Gabe. You're safe here."

Was he? Could they guarantee that?

Layke stood. "I will search the rest of the cabin just to make sure."

Exactly her thoughts. "Check the back door, too. I'll stay with Gabe."

He exited the room.

"Do you want to pray with me?" Hannah asked.

"Yes."

She got up, turned the lighthouse lamp on and flicked off the overhead light, dimming the room. She sat back down. "That's better. How about you close your eyes?"

He obeyed.

She took his little hands in hers. "Father, be with Gabe right now. Help him to go back to sleep knowing he's in Your hands. Protect us and help us to have a good night's sleep. Amen."

The wind howled as if in response to her pleading prayer. She smiled.

They could still rejoice through the storms.

Why couldn't she find joy through her current turmoil? Was she that terrible a Christian to allow doubts to creep in? She needed to give herself a stern lecture, but right now she had to focus on the boy.

Gabe opened his eyes. His earlier wild expression had disappeared and he now looked peaceful.

Thank You, Lord.

Moments later, Layke returned and sat on the bed. "All's clear. No signs of anyone."

"Mr. Layke, can you tell me a story?" Gabe asked.

Layke snapped his gaze to hers, his eyes widening. "But we don't have any books."

He'd never made up a story before?

She reached over and grabbed his hand, ignoring the spark from the simple touch. "Use your imagination."

He grinned and squeezed her hand. "I'll try."

She pulled away and folded her arms. Anything to take her mind off the electricity surging between them. Or was it just *her* imagination?

Layke stared at the ceiling. "Let me think. Hmm… where shall I start?" He snapped his fingers. "I know. Once upon a time…"

Gabe giggled. A sound she now loved. How had she become attached to this boy so quickly?

"Once upon a time, a young knight named Richard the Lionheart mounted his horse and—"

"What color was his horse?" Gabe asked.

Layke tapped his chin. "White like Shadowfax in *Lord of the Rings*."

"I love that movie." Gabe's eyes sparkled in the dim lighting.

Hannah smothered a grin. She also loved the Tolkien series.

"Me too, sport. The young knight mounted Shadowfax and galloped across the kingdom in search of the missing princess, Marian."

Hannah snorted. "Marian and Richard? Is this a Robin Hood story?"

Layke shrugged. "Only names I could think of. Stop interrupting." He winked and turned back to Gabe.

A thought raced through Hannah's mind. If only this moment would last.

"Princess Marian had been missing for two days and the King had offered her hand in marriage to the knight who rescued her, so he was determined—"

"What does determined mean?"

"Resolved."

Gabe wrinkled his face.

"Serious. Strong willed." Hannah punched Layke in the arm. "Use words an eight-year-old can understand."

"Knight Richard was *serious* and wanted to win Marian's hand in marriage. After all, he'd been in love with her since the second grade. She was the reason he became a knight. To protect her and her father's kingdom." Layke scrunched his face. "But Knight Arthur had caught Marian's attention with all his wins in the competitions."

"I don't like Arthur." Gabe crossed his arms.

"Richard didn't either, so he snuck out of the kingdom and went to search for Marian. Shadowfax galloped across the field under the cover of night."

"Was he scared?" Gabe asked.

"No. He was a brave knight." He poked Gabe. "Brave like you."

Hannah's hand flew to her chest. The man and boy before her that had been thrust into her life unexpectedly had captured her heart. What would she do when this case was over and she had to say goodbye to both?

"Richard rounded a long bend and Shadowfax reared to a stop. Richard drew his sword." The excitement in Layke's voice filled the room.

Gabe pulled the covers over his head.

She held her breath to find out what would happen next in the medieval tale.

"A scream filled the night and Richard recognized the voice. 'Marian,' he yelled. 'Richard?'" Layke mimicked a high-pitched voice. "'Watch out for the dragon,' she warned."

Gabe threw the cover off again. "What happened?"

"I'm getting to that." Layke threw his hands into the air and waved them. "Suddenly, a huge winged dragon swooped over him. He ducked as fire shot out from the creature's mouth. Richard grabbed his bow and unleashed a deadly arrow. It pierced into the beast's belly and the dragon spiraled to the ground. Richard jumped off Shadowfax and ran over to it, plunging his sword into the heart. Marian came running from her hiding place and hugged Richard. 'You saved me.'" Once again, Layke changed to a female's voice.

Hannah turned her gaze back to Gabe and found his eyes closed. He'd fallen asleep. She touched Layke's arm. "I guess you'll have to finish the story tomorrow," she whispered.

Layke stood. He pulled the covers up again to Gabe's neck. "He's so cute."

"Loved your story. You'll make a great father one day."

He snapped his head in her direction, the muscles in his neck protruding. "Not me. Never." He raced from the room.

What had just happened?

Why had she spoiled the moment? Layke trampled into his room at the end of the hall and flicked on the light. No, he would never be a father. Not that he would ever hit a child like his mother had, but he couldn't take the chance. What if his pent-up anger surfaced at an unexpected time? He'd always been able to curb it with working out and chasing down criminals.

He plunked himself on the bed. Its head- and footboards

were made from cedar planks with matching night tables. He ran his hand over the quilted cover with pictures of deer, bears and moose. The lamps were made from antlers. Thankfully, no mounted deer heads were anywhere to be seen or he'd be sleeping on the couch.

A soft knock sounded. "Layke, I'm sorry. I didn't mean anything by the comment." Hannah whispered from the other side of the door.

He slumped lower. He shouldn't have taken his anxiety over his mother's actions out on her. He sighed, got up and opened the door a crack. "It's not your fault. I'm sorry."

"Do you want to talk about it?"

An urge to bare all about his past overtook him, but he held back. Why?

Trust.

There's that word again. Why did he have such a hard time opening up?

"No. I'm heading to bed. You should, too, as we have a big day ahead of us."

A vacant stare flickered over her pretty face and then disappeared.

He'd disappointed her. Again.

"I'll see you in the morning." She put her head down and shuffled toward her room.

Nice move, Jackson.

He shut the door and silently chastised himself. She had done nothing to deserve his harsh treatment. He vowed to make it up to her tomorrow. He grabbed the packaged toothbrush and paste Hannah had left on the bed and crept to the bathroom.

Ten minutes later, he placed his gun under his pillow and climbed into bed. He prayed sleep would come quickly. He stared at the ceiling and willed his tight muscles to relax. The day had proved to be one of many tense circumstances.

His cell phone buzzed. He rolled over and grabbed it from the nightstand. He eyed the screen. Tucker Reed, a constable from New Brunswick. Why would he be calling at this hour? It was well into the wee hours of the morning in the East coast. Something was up. "Hey, bud. How are you?"

Layke had met Tucker at the police college he had attended with Hudson.

"I'm good. Just felt led to call you. Are you okay?" His Maritime accent was strong.

Layke hadn't heard from him in months. Why now? "What do you mean?"

"God put you on my heart."

Man, not him, too. "I'm fine." His throat constricted, revealing to himself he was anything but fine. "Working on a case in the Yukon."

"Really? Why there?"

Layke fluffed his pillow and leaned against the headboard. "It's a child-smuggling ring and my half brother's son has been kidnapped, so I requested my sergeant send me here to head up a joint task force to catch the gang."

Tucker whistled. "I didn't know you had a brother."

"Long story." And he was exhausted.

"I'll let you go. I wanted to let you know I'm praying for you."

He was surrounded, but right now he'd take it. "Hope the big guy listens to you."

"He always does, Layke. We just need to be still to hear His voice. Stay safe, bud." He punched off.

Why can't I hear You?

Layke threw the phone on the night table and stared at the ceiling as the wind slammed branches against his bedroom window. A thought lodged in his brain.

Was God really watching over them?

Cries sounded in between the howls of wind and Layke's thoughts. He sat up and listened. There it was again.

Hannah? He got out of bed and tiptoed to her room, edging his ear to the door.

Sure enough. Sobs came in between gasps of air.

He raised his knuckles to knock on the door and then hesitated. Had he caused this?

Now he really did need to make up for his foul mood. Maybe he'd make everyone breakfast in the morning.

He walked back to his room and climbed into bed, praying sleep would come quickly. His exhausted body needed to recuperate. However, his mind raced with possible scenarios on how the ring smuggled the children across the border. Had they all been abducted in Alaska? Was this a joint American-Canadian gang? Questions scrambled in his brain and he could not turn it off. Finally, after watching the clock on the nightstand flip to midnight, Layke drifted off.

He woke to the sound of glass breaking and bolted upright. A breeze whistled into the room, chilling him. The time now showed five in the morning and the storm still raged outside. The branch protruding into the room from the broken window proved it. His cell phone buzzed and he checked the caller. Elias. Why would he be calling and why did his head pound so much?

Layke clicked on the call. "What's up, Elias?"

"You need to get out of there now. We were just alerted to chatter on the dark web. The price on your heads increased and the location of the cabin is compromised. How, we don't know." The corporal's tone was urgent.

Layke threw off the comforter and placed his feet on the floor. His head spun as the scent of rotten eggs wafted into his room. He jumped up despite his dizziness. They had a propane leak and had to get out fast. "Elias, get the fire department here as fast as you can." He disconnected.

A question raced through Layke's mind as he stumbled to the door.

Was it an accident or intentional?

Pounding woke Hannah. Not only the pounding on the door, but in her head, too.

"Wake up, Hannah! We need to get out of here. Now!" Layke's baritone voice boomed undeniable urgency.

Something was wrong. She jumped out of bed and stumbled from the wave of dizziness plaguing her. She leaned against the wall to regain her balance. What was that horrible smell?

She stuffed her cell phone into her sweatpants and grabbed her gun before yanking open the door. "What's going on?"

"Propane leak and our position has been compromised. Get Gabe. We can't stay here any longer." He rushed down the hall and grabbed his parka, stuffing his radio into the pocket.

She hurried into Gabe's room and shook him awake. "Bud, we have to leave."

He blinked open his eyes. "Huh?"

She pulled off the covers. "We have to go."

"But I don't want to. I like it here." He whimpered.

Hannah coughed. Hard. The fumes were getting worse, and she'd used the final inhale from her puffer last night. She needed to get out of the cabin. Now.

"Come on, bud." She eased him from the bed so he wouldn't get dizzy like she did. "Mr. Layke is waiting for us." She ushered him down the hall where Layke had the front door open and was waiting with the boy's oversize jacket.

"Hurry, it's getting unbearable." He shoved a glove into Gabe's hand. "Put this over your mouth, sport." Layke wrapped the parka around the boy and lifted him.

The winds whirled into the entryway, chilling them.

Strong fumes hissed from the stove. Had someone cut the line? How had they gotten into the cabin undetected? She glanced around her friend's oasis and prayed it would be saved.

Layke nudged her toward the door. "Come on!"

She snatched her parka from the coat hook and raced into the night. The light above the door illuminated their way through the darkness.

Frigid temperatures sliced through her attire and she scrambled to get her jacket on. "Where will—"

An explosion cut off her words and rocked the cabin's structure, propelling the trio off the front porch. They fell into a mound of snow.

Layke jumped up and dragged her and Gabe farther down the laneway. "We need to move. That was the propane tank and—"

A second blast turned the cabin into a fireball and slammed a gush of heat in their direction as debris pelted them. Pieces of split timber flew into the air.

Layke shoved Gabe toward her and scrambled on top, using his body to shield both of them. His weight constricted her breathing and she struggled for air. She fought to gain control as terror surged through her body. *God, help us!*

Gabe cried and squirmed in an attempt to get out from under them.

Layke jumped up and lifted the boy back into his arms. "Get to the car! Run, Hannah!"

Her leg stung as she jumped to her feet, but she ignored the pain and raced to the vehicle.

Layke shoved aside some of the snow around the tires before putting Gabe into the back seat. "Pray we can get out of here."

Hannah crawled in beside the boy. "Shouldn't we stay until the fire trucks come?"

Layke helped her with the seat belt. "No time. This was no accident and the assailants are probably nearby. As soon as I smelled the leak, I asked Elias to get fire trucks here. We can't wait. They're after us and won't stop looking as soon as they find out we weren't in the cabin when it exploded." He circled around the vehicle and hopped in the front seat.

Gabe sobbed.

Hannah pulled him closer. "Shh. It's gonna be okay."

She glanced out the rear window at the cabin as Layke backed the Suburban down the driveway. The flames billowed into the sky and blanketed the area with lingering wisps. The inferno smothered its victim with smoke clawing its way to the sky. How could she ever tell her friend her cabin was gone? And that it was all her fault. If only—

"It's not your fault, Hannah," Layke said. "There was no way you could have predicted the assailant's next move."

She turned back around and caught a glimpse of his eyes in the rearview mirror. Even in the dark, his piercing blue eyes spoke volumes. How did he know what thoughts raced through her mind? A tear threatened to fall, and she pinched her eyebrows in an effort to stop it. Now wasn't the time to let her emotions take over. She needed to stay in control, especially when their lives were in danger.

"How did they find us?" She had to change the subject.

"No idea, but we need a place to hide. Ideas?"

She pulled her cell phone out from her pocket and hit a speed dial number. Her call was answered immediately. "Martha, so sorry to wake you."

"Oh, my dear. No sleep for me. Elias and I have been watching the dark web to try and find out who leaked your location."

Of course she was helping. The makeshift mayor always looked after her friends. She'd been known to help out with the occasional case. She reminded Hannah of Jessica Fletcher from *Murder, She Wrote*. Always an inquisitive mind. "We need a place to hide."

The woman clucked her tongue. "Come here. Our house is off the beaten trail."

"Are you sure? We wouldn't want to impose."

"Of course, honey," Martha replied.

"You're the best. We'll be there in about thirty minutes." She hung up.

"I take it you're friends with the Bakkers," Layke said.

"The entire town is. Everybody knows everyone in the small community of Beaver Creek. We need to make—"

Bang!

"Flat! Hang on," Layke yelled.

The Suburban swerved on the snow-covered road and careened toward the river.

Hannah pulled Gabe tight against her body as she waited for the tires to hit ice.

And prayed.

Layke tightened his grip on the wheel as the vehicle lurched into the air across the small ditch. The headlights caught a glimpse of the sparkling frozen river. Not good. If he was a praying man, he would ask God *not* to part the waters, so to speak. But he doubted God would listen to him after all the negativity Layke had toward Him. Would the ice hold them?

The Suburban landed with a thud and skidded across the frozen surface. Layke braked and held his breath, waiting for the SUV to finish its deadly path.

Seconds later, the vehicle stopped several feet from the road. The flattened tires would prevent them from going farther, and now their only option was to walk back.

Gabe moaned.

"It's okay, sport. We're okay." Layke opened the door and peered at the surface. "Hannah, how long has this river been frozen?"

"Probably a few weeks. We've had frigid temperatures early this year, so that's a good thing and will help us."

So far the ice held, but they needed to move quickly. Even though the temperatures were well below freezing, he didn't trust the surface. He rubbed his chilly hands together before putting on his gloves. "I'm going to test it out, sport. I'm coming around to you."

Layke stepped onto the frozen river and inched around the vehicle. The tires were flat from debris from the explosion. He opened Gabe's door, reaching his hand out to him. "It will hold you. Come with me."

"I'm scared," Gabe said.

"Take Mr. Layke's hand, bud. He won't let you go." Hannah opened her door.

Gabe obeyed and Layke pulled out the Maglite from his parka pocket, shining it toward the highway. "Hannah, we need help. Call the Bakkers."

Hannah's cell phone rang. She glanced at the screen. "Don't have to." She hit a button. "Martha, we need help. We had a flat and—" She paused. "What? When?" Another pause. "Okay, send Doyle two kilometers south of Taryn's cabin. He knows where it is. You, too."

"What is it?" Layke asked.

"Their house was just hit. We can't stay there."

"Are they okay?"

"Yes. Elias scared them off by waving his shotgun at them. Doyle is on his way to pick us up."

Sirens sounded in the distance.

"Good, and the fire trucks are on their way. Let's head slowly toward the road. I'll shine the beam so we can see." Layke fumbled with his flashlight and it shot out of his hand, skidding across the ice. He chastised himself for being all thumbs, but his fingers were still chilled from rushing out of the cabin unprepared.

"You guys stay here. I'll get it." He inched toward the Maglite. He hated this weather. "Almost—"

Crack!

The ice splintered apart and broke, separating him from Hannah and Gabe.

Layke stumbled on the uneven surface and turned back. The Suburban's front tire slipped under water. He pointed. "Run! Get to the road!"

"Not without you," Hannah yelled.

"Get Gabe to safety. Now!"

The frozen river continued to separate from the weight of the vehicle. He took a step back toward the road.

A chunk of ice broke apart beneath him and water gushed to the surface.

His legs weakened as his heartbeat exploded in his chest. A terror he'd never faced overtook his body just as the ice divided and plunged him into the arctic waters.

The last thing he heard was Hannah yell his name. Would he ever see her beautiful face again?

SEVEN

"No!" Hannah yelled as Layke disappeared beneath the ice. *Lord, save him. What do I do?* She pulled Gabe into her arms and lifted him. Layke would want her to get the boy to safety first, so she had to choose. Gabe's life over Layke's.

The ice continued to splinter. She had to move. Now.

She raced across the ice with Gabe's sobbing body bouncing in her arms. She ignored his cries and kept going. She had to figure out how to save Layke.

The approaching sirens grew louder, giving her hope and urging her forward. The fire trucks came into view, but they would never see her in the dark. She would have to get to the road and flag them down. She slipped on the ice but regained her steps.

Seconds later, she made it to the road and set Gabe down. "Stay here. I need to get Mr. Layke help."

Hannah stumbled into the street and flailed her arms, jumping up and down. "Stop! Stop!"

The fire truck's headlights grew larger and larger.

Would they see her in time?

She continued to wave her arms.

The headlights swerved as the horn blared.

They'd seen her. *Thank You, Lord.*

The fire truck stopped and the volunteer firefighters jumped down.

A tall man rushed to her. "What's wrong?"

She pointed. "Policeman just fell through the ice. Our car had a flat. Went on the river." Her words came out jumbled. She didn't have time to explain. "You have to save him! Now!"

He turned to the others. "Get the gear. James, radio ahead to the other truck en route. Tell them to attend to the fire. We have an ice rescue." He put his hand on Hannah's arm. "You okay?"

Gabe cried out.

Hannah nodded and raced back to him, gathering the boy into her arms. "The firemen will help us, bud."

The firefighters sprang into action, flooding the area with a spotlight. Men carried ropes and other equipment to the river. A team slowly edged their way to the vehicle and then flattened to their stomachs, inching their way to where Layke had gone in.

Please God. Save him.

Would she ever get to know the handsome constable?

Her body trembled as she held Gabe closer. A wave of panic threatened to surface with an asthma coughing fit. She straightened and took several deep breaths. She had to remain calm. She didn't have her inhaler and Gabe needed her right now. *You can do this.*

Another crack echoed into the night, bringing with it a single question.

Were they too late?

Layke stirred. Someone called his name. Was that Hannah? Why was he so cold? Mumbled voices sounded, reverberating in his ears. He tried to move but his cocoon-like imprisonment prevented any maneuvering. Where was he? Tangled questions oscillated through his mind.

Then he remembered.

He'd fallen through the ice. Hannah! Gabe! Were they okay? He moaned and jerked his limbs in an attempt to sit.

"Stay calm, Layke," Hannah said in a soothing tone.

He opened his eyes. "Gabe?"

"He's okay and with Doyle right now."

"Why can't I move? Where am I?"

"You're wrapped in an aluminum blanket and in the back of an ambulance."

He cleared his scratchy throat. "How did you get me out of the ice?"

"I didn't. The firefighters rescued you. They were on their way to the cabin fire and I flagged them down. They got you out just in time and revived you." She rubbed his arm. "I'm so thankful God kept you alive."

A memory surfaced. Him treading water, and then he had started to lose consciousness when a feeling embraced him. Like he wasn't alone. Could that have been God's presence?

His unbelieving heart struggled to grasp the truth in that question.

"Me, too." His voice squeaked. "I can't—"

"How's our patient?" A paramedic climbed into the ambulance.

"Tired and cold," Layke said.

"That's to be expected. You've been through quite the ordeal." The younger man pulled out a penlight. "Keep your eyes focused on my finger."

Layke followed the paramedic's finger as he moved it up, down, left and right. "What's your name?"

"Michael. Good, your pupils are fine." Michael pulled Layke's arm out from under the blanket and felt for a pulse. "Steady. You're one fortunate man, Constable. Someone up there was looking out after you."

Not him, too.

But, for some reason, the thought calmed him. Was his hardened heart softening?

Michael placed the back of his hand on Layke's forehead. "You're starting to feel normal again."

"How long was I out?" He glanced at Hannah.

Her jaw tightened. "Long enough. You scared me."

"What time is it?" Layke asked.

Hannah glanced at her watch. "Almost six o'clock."

Layke wiggled out of the blanket and sat up, immediately regretted it and clutched his dizzy head. "They're still out there. We need to get somewhere safe."

Michael placed his hand on Layke's shoulders. "You're not going anywhere but to a hospital."

Layke grimaced. "No can do. We're being hunted by killers. I need to keep Hannah and Gabe safe." He turned to her. "We need to roll. Suggestions on where?"

She put her hand on her chest and wheezed. "We can get Doyle to take us to my place. I need to pick up another inhaler and we can get my Jeep. Your cruiser is now at the bottom of the river."

"Your place could be compromised, but we could scope it out first." Layke moved the blanket and set his feet on the ambulance floor.

Michael stood and grabbed some spare clothing from a compartment. "I have gear you can have." He set them on the gurney. "Here you go."

Hannah and Michael exited the ambulance, giving him privacy.

Fifteen minutes later, Layke stepped down from the vehicle. He leaned against the side to steady his wobbly legs.

Hannah rushed over and took him by the arm. "Maybe you should go to a hospital or clinic."

"No time. I need to reconnect with Elias."

Doyle and Gabe rushed over and Gabe hugged his legs.

"Mr. Layke, you're okay. I prayed to Jesus and asked Him to help you."

A lump formed in Layke's throat. He'd only known this boy for a day and he'd already captured his heart. Layke squatted and pulled Gabe into his arms. "Thanks, Gabe."

A rustling in the nearby trees spooked Layke, reminding him of the continued danger facing them. "Time to go. Doyle, can we make a stop at the police detachment? I lost everything in the water and need to borrow a weapon and laptop. Then to Hannah's."

The superintendent pulled his key fob from his pocket. "Let's go."

Ninety minutes later, after stopping at the detachment for supplies and a replacement weapon, they turned onto a small side road in Beaver Creek. Layke glanced over his shoulder. "So far, so good. No tail." Thankfully, it was Saturday so kids would be home safe and sound. Too bad the kidnapped kids weren't. An urgency crept up his neck. He needed to concentrate on the case.

He rubbed his still chilled arms. "Hannah, how long have you lived in Beaver Creek?"

"Two years. I used to live in Whitehorse, but Doyle had me transferred here to help out with staff changes. I love the small-town atmosphere and I'm content to stay."

Doyle? How close was she to the superintendent? Surely not…no, none of his business. Layke glanced at the superintendent's profile. He had to be at least fifteen years older than her. "How did you guys meet?"

"We met on duty at the Whitehorse International Airport, right, little one?" Doyle said as he flicked on his signal light.

"Yes, you immediately gave me a hard time. I had just graduated from the CBSA and taken the Whitehorse assignment. I got it easily since not too many of the BSOs wanted to move here."

"What's a BSO?" Gabe asked.

Layke turned from the front seat to see how she'd respond.

Hannah straightened the boy's jacket and pinched his nose.

It was obvious how much she loved kids.

Something they didn't have in common.

"It's a border services officer," she said. "That's what I am."

"What do you do?"

"I watch people come across the border and make sure they don't bring anything into Canada they shouldn't."

"Like me," he said in a soft voice.

What? Layke stole a quick glance. Gabe lowered his head. "What do you mean, sport? I thought you lived at the group home near here."

"I do, but we were in Alaska for our retreat."

Layke eyed Hannah. Her taut expression revealed her anger.

The boys had been kidnapped and smuggled across her border. On her watch.

Doyle stiffened in the driver's seat. "Gabe, do you remember how they got you back into Canada?"

Layke could only guess the horror this young boy and the others went through. He took a breath to repress the anger bubbling inside.

"It was black, but I remember them putting us in boxes."

"Did they lift the boxes into a truck?" Hannah asked.

"Yes and it was stinky."

"Gabe, can you remember if the truck was big and noisy? Do you know what a transport truck is?" Layke asked.

"It stunk like the ocean."

A fish truck. Their first lead.

But how many fishing companies were there in the Yukon-Alaskan area?

They had to narrow it down.

And fast.

Hannah squeezed Gabe's shoulder. He was a smart boy to remember these details and give them their first hint of how the assailants smuggled the children across the border. She knew some of the local fisherman. It was a popular sport here in the wintertime. People travelled far to come ice fishing. She glanced out the window, mesmerized by the snow-covered trees as Doyle took the back way through their seventy-something-resident small community. She'd love to take time to play in the snow with Gabe and Layke. Build a snowman, have a snowball fight. Maybe even build a fort. However, their perilous situation prevented that from happening. It appeared they'd escaped their captors once again, but it was only by the grace of God.

Doyle pulled up to the small two-bedroom bungalow she rented. The cozy one-level timber home had ample room to make her comfortable and allowed her to host her church group every other week. She'd become attached to the sweet people of this town.

"Thanks, Doyle." She grabbed the handle.

"Wait." Layke opened his door. "I need to ensure it's safe. Give me your keys."

She fished them out of her parka and handed them to him.

"You have an alarm set?" Layke asked.

She tilted her head. "In Beaver Creek? No need for it. Some residents don't even lock their doors."

"Do you?"

"Of course. You can't take the Ontario city girl out of me. I saw too much growing up not to lock my doors."

"Good. Be right back." He climbed from the vehicle and

trudged through the deep snow to the front door, scanning the area. He opened her door and stepped inside.

"Why is he going in without us?" Gabe asked.

"Just to make sure no one is in there."

"You mean the man with the spiked hair?"

Doyle reached around and squeezed the boy's shoulder. "Yes, and any of his men."

Couple minutes later, Layke reappeared and waved them in.

She unfastened Gabe's seat belt. "Let's go. Hurry." She turned back to Doyle. "Thanks for driving us. Can you look into local fish trucks and get back to me?"

"Will do. You can't stay here. Where will you go?"

"Not sure yet."

"Let me know. Stay safe, little one."

They stepped out of the vehicle and Doyle drove off.

"Yoo-hoo! Miss Hannah!"

Hannah turned to find her neighbor, Birdie Wood, waving her newspaper in the air and making her way toward them. *Great. What did she want?* Even in the darkness, this woman didn't miss a thing. She was sweet but could be somewhat of a busybody. She knew everyone's business in the entire town. She was often seen camping out at the local restaurant nursing an endless cup of coffee while she talked to the residents and any tourists passing through.

"Hi, Birdie. How are you?'

Her long flannel nightie peeked out from under her parka. "Where have you been, missy?" She eyed Gabe. "And who's this young man?"

"Birdie, I've been working." She refrained from sharing further details as she didn't need the entire community knowing their plight. "This is Gabe. Gabe, this is Miss Wood."

Gabe puckered his face. "Why are you wearing your pajamas?"

"It's early. Came out to get my newspaper and saw you coming."

Hannah's front door opened and Layke stepped onto her tiny porch. "Hannah, you need to come inside. Now."

Right. She couldn't linger in the open.

Birdie put her hands on her hips. "Is that your boyfriend?"

"No. This is Constable Layke Jackson. Layke, this is my neighbor, Birdie."

"Hi there. Sorry to interrupt, but we have some business to attend to and must get going."

Birdie cupped her hand on her mouth as if telling Hannah a secret. "Yippie doodle! He's handsome. I think you should date him." She said it loud enough for Layke to hear.

He smirked.

Gabe giggled.

Hannah cleared her throat. "You need to turn up your hearing aid, Birdie. We gotta run." She grabbed Gabe's hand and headed toward the door.

"Tootles, everyone. Chat later." Birdie waved and ran back into her house.

Hannah and Gabe followed Layke inside the bungalow. The cheerful open concept of the living room and kitchen usually calmed her after a long shift, but not today, with a gang hot on their heels. They needed to get in and out quickly.

"I see your Jeep out back. Why didn't you take it to work yesterday?" Layke stood watch at the front window.

"Doyle picked me up."

He turned. "Does he normally?"

"Sometimes when we're on shift together. He tends to baby me, and when he heard the storm was coming, he offered to drive." She rummaged through her kitchen drawer and looked for the puffer. Her breathing had worsened and she needed it right away. After reaching toward the back, her fingers finally grasped it. She administered two puffs and stuffed it in her pocket.

"We gotta roll."

Gabe plunked himself on her plush couch. "I want to stay here. I'm hungry."

"Sport, the gang might know where Miss Hannah lives. We need to leave soon."

Hannah grabbed her keys. "Where to?"

Layke pulled out the new cell phone Constable Yellow-head had given him at the detachment. "Let me make a call. Can I go into one of your rooms?"

"Are you sure you're okay?"

He rubbed his chin. "I'm feeling much better."

She wasn't sure if she believed him or not. His skin still looked ashen, and even though she'd only known him for a day, she guessed he wouldn't let her baby him. "Second door on the right."

"Would you like a Pop-Tart?" Hannah said after Layke was gone. She could at least provide Gabe that much of a breakfast—even though it wasn't a healthy one.

"Yes!" He jumped up and down.

She opened her cupboard and pulled out a box. "Here you go." She handed him a chocolate one and stuffed more in a nearby backpack. She looked through her other food supplies and added granola bars just in case they couldn't get to a restaurant.

Hannah's cell phone played the tin whistle tune from the *Lord of the Rings*. She'd chosen the popular tune for her friend Kaylin Poirier's number. She fished her phone out of her pocket, pressing Answer. "Hey, friend. What's up?"

"Do you have a sec? I have news."

Hannah heard excitement in her friend's voice. "What's going on?"

"Hudson and I set a date. October third."

"Yes!" She pumped her fist in the air. "I'm so happy for you."

"Will you be my maid of honor?"

A phrase stuck in her head. *Never a bride, always a bridesmaid.* Would she ever get to be a bride? No. She couldn't have children, so she would never marry. Sadness washed over her. "Of course! I can't believe you're getting married to the man of your dreams." Her soft voice betrayed her feelings.

"You'll find someone, Hannah. I just know God has a plan."

Yeah, but He changed the plan.

A commotion sounded in the background. "I gotta run. My shift is starting. Stay safe."

"Love you to the moon and back." The saying they'd adopted since meeting on the streets of Windsor.

"You too." She hung up.

Layke walked back into the living room. "That Doyle?"

"No, my friend asking me to be her maid of honor on October third."

"Kaylin Poirier?"

Hannah's jaw dropped. "You know her?"

"I'm best friends with Hudson. He asked me yesterday to be his best man."

"No way!" What were the odds? "Small world. I didn't know you were from Windsor."

"Grew up there and met Hudson when I was a teenager."

"In school?"

His eyes clouded. "No. Long story."

Another part of his past he obviously didn't want to talk about. She'd let it go. For now. Her inquisitive mind needed to know more. "What did you find out?"

"Murray has agreed to let us come to his place."

"Where is it?"

"About an hour from here. Deep in the woods."

"Does he like to hide from civilization?"

He grinned. "He has an outdoor excursion company."

"Oh. Do you mean Murly's Wild West Adventures?"

"Yes. You've heard of it?" Layke checked his watch.

"Never been there, but I've read great reviews on it. Always wanted to check it out." She stuffed more into the backpack. "Do you think we'll have time to go to Tiki's Tourist Trap?"

"Who now?"

"The town's favorite eatery." The food there always made her mouth water. Just thinking about it right now made her tummy rumble.

"Not sure we—"

The front window exploded and a rock thudded on the floor.

Gabe screamed.

Seconds later, a hissing canister followed, with smoke steaming from it as it spun.

They had nano seconds before the teargas would take effect. Layke scooped Gabe up, lifted him over his shoulder and motioned to Hannah. "Back door. Run!" The smoke had already begun to burn his eyes, but he refused to rub them. That would only make it worse. "Sport, close your eyes."

Hannah put her hand over her mouth, grabbed her backpack and pulled out her Beretta before rushing to the back entrance.

Thankfully, Hannah's Jeep Cherokee was parked on the side of the house, but would they be under fire as soon as they stepped outside? Layke held tight to Gabe and also unleashed his Smith & Wesson. "Be careful. Check for any suspects. They've probably surrounded the house." And expected them to flee. Was it stupid to try? They had no choice.

Hannah wheezed, raised her gun and eased open the door. She looked around. "Looks clear, but they could be hiding in the dark."

Great, the sun wouldn't rise for probably a couple of hours. However, that could work to their advantage.

The front door crashed open. The suspects had breached the premises.

"Go now!" His voice came out low and raspy. The gas effects would consume them at any moment.

Hannah exited and unlocked her Jeep with the key fob. She kept her gun raised, searching the area for anyone lurking.

He stumbled outside as Gabe shifted in his hold, his legs still weak, but he pressed onward. Layke held him tighter with his left arm and ran to the vehicle, holstering his weapon. He climbed into the back with the boy. "You drive."

She hopped in the front and started the Jeep, backing out of the driveway just as a masked man came around the side.

He fired, but his shot went wide.

"Go! Go! Go!" Layke yelled as he buckled Gabe.

She pulled onto the street and the Jeep lurched forward at full speed.

He looked behind and saw under the light of her front door two masked men jump into their truck. They followed in hot pursuit.

"We got a tail. Step on it."

A shot hit the right-hand side mirror.

The Jeep jerked at her acceleration and he fell backward into the seat. He fastened his seat belt and reached for his radio. "Constable Layke Jackson in need of assistance. Taking on shots."

The radio crackled. "Constable Antoine here. Where are you?"

Layke glanced out the window into the dark morning. "Just passed the post office."

"Tell them we're heading toward the AlCan Highway," Hannah said.

He relayed the information.

"On my way," Constable Antoine said. A siren pierced through the radio. "Will intercept there."

Another shot hit the bumper and the Jeep swerved.

Gabe yelled.

Their vehicle jerked side to side as Hannah fought to keep it on the icy road.

"Hang on!" She yelled as she wrenched the wheel right and sideswiped a snowbank.

Layke bounced and hit his head on the window. Pain registered, but he fought to suppress it and tugged a crying Gabe closer to him. "It's okay, sport. God's got this." Had he just said that? Hudson said it all the time.

"Sorry!" Hannah pulled the Jeep back to the road and turned onto the highway.

The truck followed as another shot rang out and hit the back end. How long before they incapacitated them?

Sirens and flashing lights appeared as Constable Antoine's Suburban lurched onto the highway, crashing into the truck.

Layke peered behind them. The truck stopped momentarily and jerked around before heading in the opposite direction. *Good job, Constable Antoine.* "Pull over, Hannah."

She obeyed and veered the Jeep to the right.

"Stay with Gabe." Layke got out and headed toward the dented Suburban.

Constable Antoine maneuvered the cruiser to the side and spoke into his radio before exiting. "Only got a partial plate before the truck sped off. Alaska plates. I've called it in. You okay?"

"Good. The boy is a little shaken. The assailants breached

Officer Morgan's house with teargas. We barely got out in time." Layke rubbed the goose egg forming on his forehead from his slam into the window.

"First they compromise your hideout at the cabin and now here? How do they know where you are?" The officer took off his hat and scratched his head.

"No idea." The question had also raced through Layke's mind. A limited number of people knew their whereabouts. Could it be a mole? Dare he even think that? He knew it could happen, but in the little time he'd spent in the Yukon, the people seemed genuine.

"I know what you're thinking. Our detachment is tight-lipped. It's not us."

"Not saying it is, but it's too much of a coincidence for me. Someone is leaking information." Layke took his notebook from his jacket pocket. "Listen, did you have anything to report on the injured assailant?"

"No. So far he hasn't turned up at any hospital."

"You check local vets?"

He shook his head. "Closest vet is in Whitehorse."

Five hours away. Would they go that far? "What about medical centers?"

"Closest is the Beaver Creek Health Center on the Alaska Highway. Nothing so far."

"Okay, keep me updated and let me know what you find on that license plate. Any word on the attackers at the corporal's house?"

"Nothing."

"Okay, thanks. We need to go." He turned to leave.

"Where will you go?" Constable Antoine said.

Layke stopped. Could he trust this officer? The rule book in his head told him he needed to convey the information, but his gut told him to hang tight. Why was he following his gut all of a sudden? "Best no one knows."

The officer pursed his lips and climbed back into his vehicle.

Layke had annoyed the local police, but it couldn't be helped.

He trusted no one at this point.

EIGHT

Layke brushed aside his growing trepidation over a possible mole and opened Hannah's door. "I'll drive." He glanced at Gabe in the back seat. The boy's gaze darted back and forth as if checking for the masked men. His agitated state was evident. Layke nodded toward him and turned his eyes back to Hannah. "He needs a mother figure right now."

She looked down before he could read her expression.

What was that about? He'd like to hear more of her story but didn't have time at the moment. They needed to take cover.

Hannah stepped out of the car and climbed into the back seat without a sideways glance at him.

He winced but ignored her sudden change of mood and moved to the driver's seat. He punched Murray's address into his phone's GPS and hit Get Directions. Once Hannah buckled herself in, he pressed Go and pulled onto the highway. It would take just over an hour to get to his half brother's place. Perhaps the distance would put the enemy behind them for good, and they could concentrate on who this gang was and where they were located. He could only hope.

He glanced over his shoulder. "Sorry, we won't be able to go to Tiki's Tourist Trap today."

"I grabbed some food before we had to leave." She held up her backpack. "You want a chocolate chip granola bar or roasted almond? Pop-Tart?"

"Ahh…no. Almond bar please." He grinned and checked the rearview mirror for any tails, but only a hint of the rising golden sun stared back at him from behind a snowcapped mountain. Breathtaking. He could get used to this. Then again, he'd have to get used to the darkness and bone-chilling cold.

Hannah dangled a granola bar in front of him. "Watch out!"

He turned his gaze back to the road to see a timber wolf dart across the highway. He swerved in time to avoid the beast. An oncoming car blared his horn. Layke pulled back into his lane.

"That was close," Hannah said.

Stupid, Layke. Pay attention. You're not used to these roads. "Sorry. Can you open the bar?"

He heard rustling before she once again reached over the seat and handed it to him.

"Thanks." He took a bite and swallowed. "Sport, close your eyes and take a nap. It will be a bit before we get to Murray's. You too, Hannah."

"I'm okay. I'm more worried about you. You were just pulled out of freezing waters not that long ago. I should be driving."

He couldn't argue there. He was tired but needed to stay in control of this situation. He'd rest tonight.

An hour and a half later, his GPS directed him to take the next right, which would put him on a back road to his half brother's ranch. Good thing Hannah's Jeep had reliable winter tires as the road was barely passable with yesterday's storm. They crunched as he drove over the packed snow. Deer grazing in the field caught his attention before a host of huskies raced toward them, barking at their sudden appearance. They stopped at the side. Murray's dogs. The creatures were gorgeous.

Gabe popped up in the back seat. "Oh, goody. I love dogs." He pointed. "Look at them all!"

"They pull the sleds," Hannah said.

"Can I go on a ride?"

"We'll see, sport." Layke drove the Jeep into the driveway and his jaw dropped. The two-story log home housed a circular bay window on the ground level with a balcony above it and a stone chimney off to the left. A matching log structure was attached to the right and appeared to be some type of added room. An office perhaps?

Hannah whistled. "Wow, this place is gorgeous."

"I know, right?" He parked the Jeep beside a van with the sign Murly's Wild West Adventures on the side along with a picture of a husky.

The front door opened and Layke took a breath. This was his first face-to-face meeting with his recently discovered half brother. He'd only Skyped with him a few times after their initial contact.

The burly, bearded man dressed in Buffalo plaid stepped onto the entrance veranda. He waved.

Layke hesitated. Could he face the son of his criminal father? The father he never knew as a child and only found out about from an ancestry test?

Hannah squeezed his shoulder. "You okay?"

He drew in a ragged breath. "I will be."

"You haven't met Murray before, have you?"

He turned in his seat. Was he that much of a giveaway? He needed to curb his emotions. After all, he was a cop with all the rules. *Never let them see how you really feel* popped into his head. He'd gone this long without revealing his past. He could do this. "Only on Skype."

"How did you find each other?" Hannah unbuckled Gabe's seat belt.

He glanced back at Murray. "Long story and we don't have time right now." He knew his voice held a curtness to it. Would she let it go?

"Fine." She opened her door and reached for Gabe. "Shall we go meet some dogs, bud?"

Why was he so rude? It was an honest question. He shook his head and climbed out of the Jeep.

Six barking dogs bounded up the driveway.

"Boys! Stop." Murray's brassy voice commanded attention.

They stopped immediately. Their barking ceased.

Wow. Layke was impressed with the well-trained animals. He stepped toward his half brother and held out his hand. "Nice to meet you in person."

Murray pulled him into a bear hug instead. "None of this handshake nonsense. We're family."

A wave of emotion clotted in his throat. Family? How long had he yearned for someone to be *his* family? Too long. He swallowed to suppress the tangled feelings racing through him. After all, he had a job to do. Find those boys and stop the smuggling ring. Layke stepped back from Murray's embrace, resolved to do just that and not let his own remorse impede his investigation. His rules took over once again.

The door opened and a petite brunette stepped outside. She wrapped her fleece coat tighter.

Murray motioned toward her. "Layke, this is my wife. Natalie."

She hugged him. "Nice to finally meet you."

"Sorry for the circumstances."

"You need to find my boy." Tears filled her hazel eyes.

"I'm working on it."

Gabe bounded up beside him and hugged his leg. "Murray, Natalie, this is Gabe." He turned to Hannah. "And this is border patrol officer Hannah Morgan."

They shook hands.

Gabe jumped up and down. "Can I have a ride on your doggie's sled?"

"Sport, let's get to know them first, okay?"

Murray whistled and the dogs surrounded them within seconds. "Boys, meet Gabe."

One dog rubbed up against Gabe and licked his hand. The boy giggled and patted him. "They're cute."

Hannah rubbed the one beside her. "What type of husky are they?"

"Siberian," Murray said.

"They're gorgeous." Hannah petted another one. "They have such beautiful blue eyes."

Natalie pointed to one sitting off to itself. "We have one girl. Check out Saje. She's special."

Gabe walked over and yelled back. "She has two colors. Blue and brown."

Murray laughed. "That's right. Some huskies do." He pointed to the entrance. "Let's get you inside. The temps today are brutal."

He wasn't wrong. Even though the sun had come out, the frigid air formed ice crystals that danced along the front of the log home. If it wasn't so cold, Layke would almost enjoy the sight before him and the sparkling field to the right of the building. Almost.

The group followed Murray into the house and a wave of heat rushed at Layke, followed by the smell of a bonfire. Made sense that this outdoor man would have a real wood-burning fireplace. It was exactly what Layke needed. After today's ordeal all he wanted to do was sit beside a roaring fire.

"You can leave your coats and boots here. Let's head to the family room." Murray pointed in the direction he wanted them to go.

They hung their parkas on the wooden antler-style coat-rack and followed the couple.

Layke stepped into a rustic-themed living room similar to Hannah's friend's cabin. The only difference was the plaid-decorated furniture.

Gabe passed them and ran to the stone hearth. "Can we have s'mores?" He clapped. "Please?"

"Sport, not now. We just got here." He pointed to the red-and-navy-plaid couch. "Take a seat."

Hannah roamed the room, peering at the decor with her mouth gaping open. "This place is beautiful."

"Thanks," Natalie said.

Layke moved to an end table displaying family pictures. One of Murray and Natalie with a young boy in the middle caught his attention. "Noel?"

Murray rubbed his short beard and clenched his jaw. "Yes."

Gabe popped up. "Wait. I know him."

"From where, sport?"

Tears pooled and he stumbled backward. "The other boys in the cave."

A simultaneous gasp filled the room, silencing the crackling fire and chilling him through to the bones.

Hannah raced over to Gabe and threw her arms around him. "We've got you, bud." She guided him to the oversize plaid couch. "Tell us about Noel."

"Gabe, are you sure it's him?" Layke sat on the opposite side and put the photo he'd taken from the table in front of Gabe.

"Yes, but he looks better in this picture."

Murray knelt in front of them. "What do you mean, son?"

"He looks happy. He's sad now."

Natalie fell to the floor and sobbed. Her husband rushed over and took her into his arms, rocking her.

Hannah's chest tightened and she clutched her abdomen. This mother obviously ached for her son's return as Hannah longed for a child of her own. She couldn't have one, but resolution snapped her into a straightened position. She would find Noel and the other kids if it claimed her own life. *Lord, give us insight and guidance.*

"Sport, what else can you tell us?" Layke's softened voice and contorted face revealed his own determination to find Noel.

The fire snapped as they waited for Gabe's answer.

"He cries a lot. One of the men touched his arm to try and get him out of bed, and Noel screamed and kicked." Gabe wrung his hands together. "The bad men came and took him away. I think to another room. I haven't seen him since."

"How long ago?" Layke asked.

"The day before I left. We need to get him help." Gabe jumped up. "Why does he cry all the time?"

Murray guided his wife to a wooden rocking chair and stood beside her. "He has autism."

"What's that?"

"A disorder where Noel has a hard time being with other people." Hannah pulled him back onto the couch.

Gabe wrinkled his nose. "I didn't like to see him cry."

Natalie sobbed.

"Sport, how did you get away?" Layke asked.

"I snuck out when the lady wasn't looking."

"The one you mentioned before?"

Gabe nodded. "She went to get a book to read to me and I ran out the door. I wanted to see if I could get help for my friends. For Noel."

"Why didn't you grab a coat?" Hannah asked.

"The bad men were coming down the hall and I didn't have time. I ran." He sniffed.

Hannah pulled out a tissue from a box on the coffee table and handed it to him. "Where were the rest of the boys?"

"Still at the cave. I pretended I was sick, so I could stay at the ranch."

"Where were you?" Murray put another log on the fire and used the poker to move the coals around.

Layke stood. "They blindfolded the boys, but we know they're at a ranch somewhere close as Gabe escaped and ran to the CBSA station in Beaver Creek."

Murray's eyes flashed. "Why aren't you and the local authorities searching the area then?"

Layke shoved his hands in his pockets. "Other constables are. The gang is after Gabe and Hannah, so we needed to hide."

"Why are they after them?" Natalie said in between sobs.

Hannah got up and took Natalie's hands in hers. "We both can identify one of them. I promise we'll find Noel."

Layke cleared his throat.

She glanced at him and noted his tightened expression directed at her. The rules man once again emerged. He wouldn't promise anything, but she had to give this mother hope. "We will do everything within our power to bring this gang to their knees."

Natalie bit her lip.

An idea formed. Something that would hopefully make her feel useful. "Natalie, could you take Gabe and get him cleaned up? He's been in these dirty clothes for who knows how long and could use something fresh. Is Noel the same size?"

Natalie stood. "Close. I will also find you both something to wear."

"Thank you."

Natalie reached for Gabe's hand. "Come with me, and maybe later we'll take you out and play with the dogs."

Gabe's expression brightened, and he hopped alongside her as they left the room.

Murray plunked himself into the rocker. "Thank you for doing that. The distraction will do her good. I'm sorry for my harsh reaction earlier. We're just sick with worry. Noel needs his parents to help calm him. I should never have sent him on that trip. What kind of father am I?" He buried his head in his hands.

Layke walked over and squeezed his shoulder. "You can't think like that, man."

"I know, but it's hard not to."

Layke sat in the chair beside him. "Question. Where was Noel's retreat located?"

"Near Anchorage, Alaska. Why?"

"So, not in Canada? Interesting." He turned to Hannah. "Seems to be the kidnapper's MO. Abduct the kids in Alaska and smuggle them across the border. Probably all in fish trucks, too."

"I wonder why they'd risk getting caught coming back into Canada? Why not grab them here?"

Layke tapped his chin. "Too protected. They're exposed more at a campout. Easier access."

"Those poor kids. Makes me so angry." Hannah's cell phone buzzed in her pocket. She fished it out and glanced at the screen. Doyle. She got up. "I need to take this. My boss could have news."

She stepped out into the hall and went around the corner. She found herself in a kitchen. The decor matched the rest of the house with wood-covered counters and matching tabletops. The chairs legs were made out of logs. She pulled one out and sat. "Doyle, do you have news?"

"Are you okay?"

"Yes. We're fine. Have any of the other stations had leads?"

"Still working on it."

She sighed and fingered the wooden fruit bowl in front of her. "We need to find these kids. Layke's nephew has autism and isn't coping away from his parents."

"Sorry to hear that. Mike from Little Gold Creek may have a lead soon. Just waiting to hear back from him. Where are you?"

"Murly's Wild West Adventures." She explained their location and about Layke's family. "Please keep that under your hat. We're still not sure how the gang keeps finding us."

"Will do."

"Any word on the fishing trucks? I can't believe that's how the boys were smuggled across the border." She clenched her fist. "They must have put them among fish. This is outrageous."

"I know, little one. I'm waiting on a call from a local fisherman. Gotta run. Stay safe."

She smiled at the older man's concern in his voice. He'd been like a father to her over the past five years. She couldn't have gotten through her move to the Yukon without his guidance and support.

Her cell phone pinged an alert and she checked the screen. An interoffice CBSA communication with patrol officer Madison Steele's picture popped on her screen with the caption, "New Brunswick–Maine border patrol officer involved in major bust." Hannah read more about her friend Madison's dealings in solving a case where she crippled a deadly smuggling ring. *Good for you, Madison.*

Ding!

A text from Martha appeared. U OK? Heard about Layke.

Hannah sat in a chair and composed a reply. We're OK.

Where R U?

Layke's brother's ranch. Near the old town of Snag.

Stay safe.

Hannah pocketed her phone and chuckled as she pictured sweet Martha texting with her long manicured nails. The woman surprised everyone with her many talents.

Natalie walked into the kitchen. "Gabe is all washed up and getting dressed." She put jeans and a yellow-and-black-plaid shirt on the counter. "These are for you. I gave Layke some of Murray's clothes, although they might be a little big for him." She giggled.

"You okay if I clean up?"

"Of course. Use the bathroom upstairs. Second door on the right."

Hannah squeezed the woman's arm. "Thank you. We really appreciate being able to hide here."

"It's the least we can do." She pulled hot chocolate from the cupboard. "I'm going to make Gabe a treat."

Natalie knew how to worm her way into the boy's heart. She couldn't console her son, so she'd try and lighten Gabe's load of grief. A loving mother. Something Hannah had longed for all her life.

She steeled her jaw to suppress the sudden wave of emotion, grabbed the clothes and made her way up the hardwood steps to the second level.

Twenty minutes later, she walked back into the living room and drew in a sharp breath.

Layke stood wearing jeans and a blue plaid shirt that matched his eyes.

He held her gaze as his lips curved upward. A smile guaranteed to melt her heart if she wasn't careful. Then again, who was she kidding? It already had. She shoved the thought aside and plunked herself on the sofa.

Layke's phone rang. "Jackson here." He paced. "Constable Antoine. Any news?"

Hannah held her breath.

Murray tugged at his beard.

Layke halted. "What? When? Where is that located?" He paused. "Good, we're on our way." He clicked off.

"What is it?" Hannah asked.

"The injured suspect was spotted at a health center nearby. We need to find him. He's our only lead. Constable Antoine has dispatched local police that will meet us there." He scooped up his laptop from an end table.

"Go!" Murray yelled. "We'll keep Gabe safe."

Layke touched her arm. "I need you for backup. Grab your gun."

She ignored the tingling from the simple gesture and pulled her Beretta from the back of her jeans. "Right here." She dangled her keys. "You drive."

They snatched their coats and raced out into the yard.

She jumped into the passenger seat as the dogs barked in the background. She was thankful for the protective animals. They would defend not only this precious family but the property, too.

Layke reversed the Jeep from the driveway and sped down the road, the ranch disappearing from her vision as a question lodged in her mind.

Would they make it back alive to see Gabe again?

NINE

Layke handed his cell phone to Hannah as he kept his eyes on the road. He gave her the clinic's address. "Put it into my GPS so we know where we're going. We don't have much time."

"How did we find him?" She tapped the phone.

"Constable Antoine said a nurse from the clinic was in another room when he came in and demanded they treat his wounds. She hid until she felt it safe to sneak out and called 911."

"When was this?"

"An hour ago. He can't be hurt too badly to only be seeking medical attention now."

"He probably knew better not to get treated in Beaver Creek. That the constables would look there first." She pressed the button.

The directions instructed them to stay on the road for another fifty kilometers.

Their trip would take time. Time they didn't have. A thought came to him. "Hannah, can you look up the Frontier Group Home? I want to talk to Sister Daphne."

Hannah typed on the small cell phone keyboard.

He tapped his thumb on the steering wheel. Would the sisters give them answers?

"Here we go." She dialed the number and waited. "Yes, I would like to speak to Sister Daphne, please."

She hit the speaker and placed the phone on the middle console for him to hear.

"This is Sister Daphne."

"This is Constable Layke Jackson and I have border patrol officer Hannah Morgan on the line."

"How can I help you, officers?"

"We're investigating the kidnapping of Gabe Stewart and the other boys from your group home."

A sharp inhale swept through the speaker. "Have you found them?"

"Only Gabe," Hannah said. "He's safe, Sister."

"What about the others?"

"We're still looking. What can you tell us about Gabe?" Layke swerved around a chunk of ice on the road.

"Sweet boy but shy. Doesn't open up well and takes a long time for him to make friends. His mother left him on the doorstep as a baby."

"Has anyone ever inquired about him since that time?" Hannah's softened voice was strained.

"Not at this home," the nun said. "He's been moved around a lot and feels unloved. I've tried to convince him otherwise."

Hannah turned her gaze out the window. "Is there anything you can tell us about him and the other boys who were taken that can help us narrow down why they targeted your organization?"

"No idea. Find them, please."

Layke gritted his teeth. "We will." He cringed. *There you go again, Jackson. Promising something you can't guarantee.*

"Thank you. I have to go now. It's time for the children's classes."

"We appreciate your help. If you think of anything else,

please call." Layke spieled off his cell phone number and hung up. "Well, that wasn't helpful."

"Not at all. Poor Gabe. I feel for him."

He stole a peek at her profile. Tension lined her jaw. "You okay?"

"Yup." She twirled a curl around her finger. "Your brother and his wife seem nice."

Change of conversation. She obviously didn't want to talk about what bothered her. "They do." He wished he'd known them long before today.

"How did you find out about them?"

Layke bit his lip. He knew she'd ask again. How much of his story did he want to tell her? He glanced at the woman beside him. Her wrinkled brow revealed concern. He looked away and clenched his mouth shut. He didn't need her pity.

She rubbed his arm. "You can trust me."

He suppressed a gasp and looked back at her. Had she also felt the electricity that surged through his body from her simple touch? The sudden impulse to hold her in his arms and protect her slammed him like an oncoming freight train at full speed. *Get a grip. You know you can't commit to any woman.* Especially one who clearly wants children. And he didn't.

"My mother told me she didn't know who my father was."

"What? How could that be?" She pulled her hand away.

"I'm afraid my mother wasn't a nice person. She had boyfriend after boyfriend. Said my father was none of my concern and told me to stop asking." He could still picture the anger on her face from years gone by. "A week after she warned me to stop asking, a news broadcast caught her attention. She shut off the TV and said my father was dead."

"I thought she didn't know who he was."

"She lied." He rubbed the muscles in his neck. "She lied about many things."

"How did you find Murray?"

"You know Kaylin's story, right?"

"Yes. She reconciled with her estranged father. What has that got to do with it?"

"It convinced me to look into my family, see where I might be from. So I did one of those ancestry DNA tests."

"And?"

"Found out my father was very much alive and—" He stopped. He couldn't tell her the secret he'd kept from everyone.

"What?"

"Nothing. I don't want to talk about him."

Her shoulders slumped. "Did your mother say why she lied?"

How could he explain to her how he had distanced himself from the woman when it was obvious she possessed mother-like tendencies? "I haven't spoken to her since I confronted her about my dad. She ordered me to stay away, so I hung up and refused to take any more of her calls. Changed my number."

"I'm sorry."

"I'm not." His voice came out harsh, but he'd leave it at that.

"So, how did you find Murray then?"

"I didn't. He found me. Called me out of the blue one day and told me we had the same father. I didn't believe him at first but did a check on him. Murray lived in Windsor as a teen and then moved to Whitehorse to go to college. We started Skyping together. He's like you, you know."

"What do you mean?"

"A Christian."

"Good. His faith will give him strength to battle this ordeal."

Could he believe her? Why had God abandoned him as a child? "Not sure I believe that."

"What's made you skeptical toward God?"

A mother who beat her only child. He held back the words he wanted to say. After all of these years, his disdain for her still came through. Why couldn't he let it go?

"Turn right in 500 meters," the GPS commanded.

For once, he was thankful for the voice on his GPS. It interrupted their conversation and put his head back into the game. Where it needed to be. Not in the clouds thinking of a deceitful mother and a father who'd murdered.

Layke turned right into the small community and followed the GPS instructions to the health center. Cars had jammed the tiny parking lot and the lineup at the front door indicated the clinic had not opened.

"This could be interesting. The people will be antsy after waiting in the cold for the clinic to open. We may need to do some crowd control. Do you have your badge? We'll need to identify ourselves since we're in civilian clothing." He winced as he thought about a rule he was breaking by not being in uniform, but it couldn't be helped. He parked on the side of the road and turned off the engine.

She pursed her lips and pulled out her credentials.

It was obvious she still waited for him to answer her question, but he had to concentrate on doing his job. One of his rules… *Keep your head in the game at all times.* He fastened his badge to his belt and stepped out of the Jeep.

Hannah followed in silence.

They wove their way through the line and flashed their badges.

Once they got to the front of the building, Layke stopped and waved his badge in the air. "Everyone. This is police business. Please return to your vehicles and head home. The clinic is closed for the day. Come back tomorrow."

Flashing lights and a siren announced the arrival of the local constables. Layke flinched. The sound would alert the suspect to their presence and they'd lose their advantage.

As if on cue, a shot pierced through the clinic's window.

Layke and Hannah ducked, unleashing their weapons.

"Get down!" Layke yelled.

Panic erupted and the crowd scattered like bees from a stirred nest. They knocked each other down as they ran to their cars. Engines started and cars rammed into each other as they tried to exit the parking lot.

They must contain the chaos before someone got hurt.

The constables drew their guns and crouched.

Layke waved them over. "Do you have a crowbar in case we need to breach?" Introductions would have to wait for now.

"Yes," the tall officer said. "I'll get it." He ran back to the cruiser while the other officer directed the cars out of the lot.

The constable returned and handed Layke the crowbar.

"Where in the clinic did the witness call from?" Layke asked.

"She told us she was out front. The suspect was in the back patient room with the doctor who was called into the center. They don't normally house doctors, only nurses."

"He fired from the front, so we need to assume he now has the other nurse hostage. You circle around back. We'll take the front. Be careful. This suspect is wounded and armed. Not a good combination." He pulled out his radio. "What channel are you on?"

The constable told him and rushed off.

"Hannah, I know you're trained in defensive tactics, but please stay behind me and follow my lead."

"Understood. What's the plan?"

He pulled out his cell phone. "I'm going to call inside and hope he picks up." He Googled the clinic's name and entered its number. He could hear the phone ringing from behind the glass door. He waited. Two rings. Three. Four. "Come on, pick up." Six. Seven—

"What do you want?" the rough voice blared.

"This is Constable Layke Jackson. With whom am I speaking?"

"You don't need to know. Get off the property or I'll start by shooting this pretty nurse."

Great, he had her hostage. "Listen, no one needs to get hurt. We want to help you."

He cussed. "You can help by going away!"

"Not gonna happen, man. We don't want you. We want your boss." He had just broken another of his rules… *Never misinform a suspect.* He gripped his cell phone tighter. Truth was, they did want him, too. If he had his way, everyone in this gang was going down.

Silence.

He caught his attention.

"What will you do for me?"

"Let the nurse and doctor go. Then we'll talk."

A crash sounded at the back of the clinic.

"Someone's at the rear door. I told you to stay out."

The other constable.

Layke grabbed his radio and changed the channel. "Stand down, Constable." His command was rough, but he needed the officer to obey. He was almost through to the suspect. He put his cell phone back to his ear. "I instructed the officer to stay outside."

"I don't believe you. You were warned."

Click. *Beep.* The dial tone buzzed in his ear like an annoying mosquito that wouldn't go away. He clicked off and shoved the phone into his pocket. That conversation had not gone well.

A shot from inside was followed by a woman's scream.
They had to move. Now.

"Breach on three," he yelled into his radio. He holstered
his weapon and held the crowbar tightly. "Hannah, hold
my radio to my mouth." He needed both hands to break
the glass.

She obeyed and pressed the radio button.

He moved to the side with her to his right.

"One. Two. Three. Go! Go! Go!"

A crash sounded at the back.

He slammed the crowbar into the front door, shatter-
ing the glass.

Hannah stuffed Layke's radio into her back pocket and
raised her weapon. Her pulse hammered fear through her
veins as she waited for Layke to clear the doorway. This
was the first time she'd ever been part of a breach in this
nature. Sure, she'd been trained on it but never had to
do one with living, breathing humans inside. Her duties
mostly included inspecting vehicles coming across the
border. She braced for what was about to happen.

Layke threw the crowbar aside and unleashed his gun.
"Stay behind me." He eased through the door, pointing his
Smith & Wesson in different directions.

Her boots crunched on the fallen glass, the sound
matching her thudding heartbeat. She crouched low and
mimicked Layke's posture.

Layke edged around the corner with his weapon in
front. "Police! Stand down!"

"Stay back, or I swear I'll kill her." The injured suspect inched forward with the petite blonde nurse in front
of him and a gun thrust into her side. The man's wild eyes
darted back and forth as his hand shook. His wiry red curls
peeked out from under his tuque.

The doctor sat on the floor clutching his wounded leg, blood pooling around him.

Layke took another step.

The local constable appeared in the hallway but remained hidden.

Layke raised his left fingers slightly in a stop position. "No one move."

Hannah stole a peek at the constable. Would he get the hint to stay hidden? She anchored herself beside Layke.

"Bud, the doctor is hurt. He needs attention. Let's end this." Layke took another step.

"Stop! I don't want to hurt her, but I will if I have to." He squeezed harder.

The nurse moaned.

"What's your name?" Layke asked.

"Rob."

"We don't want you, Rob. Cooperate with us and we'll let the crown attorney know you helped us." Layke inched closer.

Hannah held her breath. Would the man listen without someone else getting shot? *Lord, help us to end this situation peacefully.*

"He'll kill me if he knows I talked and, believe me, he'll know."

"Who? Your boss?"

Rob waved his gun toward Hannah. "How about we swap? You give me Hannah and I'll let you have the nurse."

Hannah flinched. How did he know her name and what did he want with her?

Layke's face twitched and he raised his gun higher. "Not gonna happen."

Hannah stepped forward into the line of fire. "Why do you want me?"

Layke reached around and pushed her back. "Behind me."

Rob tilted his head. "Oh. You're sweet on her, aren't

you? Don't blame you. She's pretty." He sneered, revealing his cigarette-stained teeth.

"I'll shoot you before I let you take her." Layke moved to the left.

Where was he going?

Rob dragged the nurse to follow Layke's stance. Out of the way of his peripheral vision of the other policeman.

Smart thinking, Layke.

The constable edged around the corner and moved behind the reception desk.

"What's your boss's name?" Layke asked.

That's it. Keep him distracted.

The constable moved out from behind the desk and inched his way forward.

Hannah once again held her breath.

"You think I have a death wish? You're dumber than I thought, Constable Jackson."

Layke shifted his stance. "What can you tell me about him?"

The man scoffed. "Let's just say the boss is everywhere and knows all about your investigation."

How? Hannah's mind raced to try to figure out how that was possible. This ring spread far if they knew their names and were able to follow their case.

"What—"

The officer hiding lunged behind Rob and knocked the gun out of his hand. He wrenched the suspect's arm up his back.

Rob yelled.

Layke raced forward and pulled the nurse away, pushing her toward Hannah.

Hannah grabbed her and removed her from the deadly situation. "You're okay. We've got you."

"Nice work, Constable. What's your name?" Layke asked.

"Taylor."

"Layke Jackson from Calgary."

Constable Taylor nodded and cuffed Rob, shoving him into a waiting chair. He spoke into his radio, telling the constable outside they were clear, and asked for an ambulance for the injured doctor.

Layke turned to the nurse. "You hurt?"

She shook her head. "Just shaken."

Hannah squeezed her shoulder. "You were brave calling us."

"The constables here will take your statement," Layke said. "Is there a room where we can question the suspect?"

"Yes, the examining room is down the hall."

Constable Taylor handed Layke the cuff keys. "In case you need them." He moved to attend to the injured doctor.

The short constable rushed into the room. "Ambulance is on its way. The crowd outside is gone."

"Good work." Layke stuck out his hand. "I'm Constable Layke Jackson. You are?"

The man returned the gesture. "Constable Brooks. Nice to meet you. Constable Antoine apprised us of the situation with the smuggling ring. How can we help?"

Layke motioned toward the woman. "Can you take the nurse and get her statement? Hannah and I will interrogate the suspect."

"Got it," the constable said.

Layke took three long strides and yanked Rob out of the chair.

"Ouch. You're hurting me," he whined.

"Not so tough now, are you?" Layke pushed him toward the hall. "How about we have a little chat?"

Hannah holstered her weapon and followed them down the corridor. They stepped inside the examining room. Soiled gauzes were piled in the sink. Beside it a bullet sat in a metal tray. They needed to collect that for evidence.

Layke removed the cuffs and then handcuffed Rob to a metal chair before leaning against the counter and crossing his arms. His stance spoke authority and that's what they needed in this makeshift interrogation room. "Tell us about this child-smuggling gang."

"I ain't telling you squat!"

Layke looked at Hannah, his eyes flashing.

She could almost read his mind. He wanted to save Noel and the other boys. And fast. Perhaps they could reason with the suspect. She stepped forward. "Rob, do you want to go down for multiple kidnappings and the possible murder of innocent children?"

His eyes widened. "What? No kids have been hurt."

"Really? I know of one in your care that is currently in bad shape without his parents."

He looked away.

"Help us save these children and the judge might be lenient on your sentencing." She hoped not but wouldn't utter those words to him.

"Do I have your guarantee?"

"We'll tell the judge you cooperated," Layke said.

That was all they could promise.

Rob shifted in his chair. "I don't know much. I only watch the boys while they're at the ranch."

"Which is where?" Hannah asked.

Silence.

"What are they mining in the cave? Gold?" Layke pulled out a notebook from his back jeans pocket.

Rob shrugged. "Don't know. Don't care. I just get paid to watch them."

This wasn't helping. "Who's the guy with spiked hair?"

"Cash."

How was that a name? "Cash what?"

"No idea."

Layke wrote a note. "Who's the leader of the gang?"

"I only know him as Broderick."

Obviously not his real name. "Tell us more. How do you pick the boys?"

"No idea."

Layke pulled up a chair and straddled it. "How do you smuggle them across the borders?"

"No idea."

Was that his answer for everything? They were getting nowhere fast. Hannah grabbed a wad of her curls and scrunched them as she paced the small room. Her motherly instinct wanted to do everything to protect these boys, but how could she do that if they couldn't find them. Wait. She spun around. "Answer my earlier question. Where is this ranch?"

Layke's cell phone buzzed. He stood and pulled it out of his pocket. "I need to take this." He stepped outside.

"Tell me, gorgeous, you have a boyfriend?"

Really? "None of your concern. For the third time, where is the ranch?" Her words came out through gritted teeth.

"I only—"

Layke came back into the room. "We gotta roll." He walked over to Rob, removed the cuffs, and hauled him from the chair. "You're going with the constables for a ride."

"What about my deal?"

"Take it up with them. Let's go." Layke pushed him out the door.

Hannah followed them outside.

The paramedics put the doctor into the back of an ambulance and raced out of the parking lot, sirens blaring. The nurse had been dismissed by the officers after they'd taken her statement. She leaned against the building talking on her cell phone.

Constable Taylor walked over and took Rob's arm.

"We'll take it from here." He put the suspect into their cruiser. Hopefully, the constables would get the location of the ranch out of the suspect. Her hopes just raised a notch. Perhaps this ordeal was almost over.

The two constables turned around before getting into the vehicle. "Where will you go next?" Constable Brooks asked.

"Just got a call that the forensic artist is en route to see Gabe. It's a bit of a drive and we need to get back there."

"Good. Stay safe. See you—"

Boom!

The cruiser exploded, sending it crashing into a parked car.

TEN

The fiery blast slammed Layke hard onto the snow-plowed parking lot. The cruiser's nonstop piercing siren throbbed in his ears. His heart jackhammered as pain coursed down his legs from the impact. He drew in a ragged breath in an attempt to stop the trepidation overtaking him. *Hannah?* He bolted into a seated position. Dizziness plagued him and he fought to bring it under control. Where was she? Was she hurt?

Layke finally spotted her a few feet away. She sat on the ground, leaning against the Jeep with her head between her hands.

"Hannah?" Layke eased himself up and took a shaky step. He stumbled over to where she sat and knelt. "Are you hurt?"

Her breathing was erratic.

He grabbed her hands and pulled them away from her face. "Look at me."

Her eyes darted back and forth, not focusing on any one thing. Blood trickled out from a cut on her temple.

"Talk to me."

"Can't breathe. Wind. Knocked. Out."

"Take a big breath. In and out. Through your mouth. Then suck in your stomach. That should help."

She obeyed, doing it a couple of times.

The constables ran over.

"Is she okay?" Constable Taylor asked.

"Got the wind knocked out of her. How about you both?"

"Just a few cuts and probably some bruises." He pointed toward the cruiser. "Rob wasn't so fortunate. Do you think he was the target?"

Layke scratched his head. "That's my guess. Not sure how they knew where we were. Maybe he contacted them before we got here?"

"Possibly. We've called the volunteer fire department for this zone and another ambulance. They should be here soon. We'll check the area for evidence and your vehicle for any tracking devices." They walked away.

Layke refocused his attention on Hannah. "Can you breathe now?"

"Yes."

He pulled a tissue from his pocket and brushed a curl off her face as he wiped the blood from her temple.

She let out a soft gasp.

Had he really just done that? Had he broken another one of his rules… *Never get close to someone during an intense situation*? He had to stop breaking these or it would cost him dearly. He pulled his hand away. "There, you're good now. Are you hurt anywhere else?"

"No. How are you? You've been through a lot today."

"I'm fine." Not really, but he wouldn't tell her that. They needed to remain focused.

Ten minutes later, an ambulance roared into the parking lot, and a male paramedic jumped out. He grabbed a bag and headed toward them. "Where are you hurt?"

Layke stood. "I'm okay. She has a cut on her temple." He helped Hannah stand.

"I'm fine," she said.

The paramedic guided her toward the ambulance. "I need to check you just to be safe."

She turned back to Layke. "But I have—"

"It's okay. I've got this." Layke waved her off.

A firetruck raced into the lot with its siren screaming and lights flashing. The firemen jumped down and quickly moved in syncopation to extinguish the blaze. Great teamwork. These volunteer firefighters knew what they were doing.

Constable Taylor approached him, holding his notebook. "We've called for the local coroner to come. We didn't find any devices on your vehicle." He glanced toward the charred cruiser. "Such a waste. Did you get any information from him?"

"Not a lot. Just the names Broderick and Cash. Hopefully, the forensic artist can get a good enough sketch from Gabe's description so we can put out a BOLO."

"We've got this covered. You can head out as soon as Hannah is done with the paramedic."

Layke held out his hand. "Thanks. Keep me updated on any information you receive?"

He returned the gesture. "Will do. Same goes for you."

They exchanged business cards.

Layke nodded and walked over to the ambulance.

The paramedic was finishing up with Hannah as he approached. "You good to go, or are they taking you to the hospital?"

"I'm fine. We need to get back to Gabe."

"Agreed."

She hopped down from the back of the ambulance. "Are we able to get any evidence from inside the health center?"

"The constables are securing the scene and will interview local residents. It's protocol."

"Good. How do you think they found us?"

"He must have called them when we arrived. I wish we could have gotten more information from him."

They walked toward her Jeep. "Yah, Broderick and Cash isn't a lot to go on. Can you check your CPIC database?"

He was impressed by her knowledge of the Canadian Police Information Centre that gives the police authorities details on crimes and offenders—a wealth of information. However, without last names, he doubted they'd find anything. "I will check on the way back to Murray's." He handed her the keys. "Do you want to drive?"

"Sure." She unlocked the vehicle and climbed in.

He pulled the police-issued laptop Elias lent him from the back seat as she maneuvered the Jeep out the side roads and onto the main highway. He peered at the sky. Dark clouds had smothered the sun and now created an ominous display. The earlier cold temperatures had warmed in a flash. Were they in for more snow or something else? He shook his head. He wasn't sure he could handle another storm after yesterday's.

Layke set the thought aside and typed the name Broderick into the CPIC search engine and waited. He glanced at Hannah's profile.

Her wavy light red locks sat just below her shoulders. He liked her hair down instead of in a ponytail, enhancing her already beautiful features. What was her story? "So, tell me. You seeing anyone?"

Her head snapped to the right and her jaw dropped. Her squinted eyes revealed her confusion at his question.

He gritted his teeth. What was wrong with him? Why did he even care? He glanced back to his screen and the circling cursor as it searched the database. The weak signal slowed his inquiry. "Sorry, none of my business."

"It's okay. I'm not seeing anyone. You?"

He stole a peek at her.

She looked back at the road.

What game were they playing? *Layke, don't get involved. You promised yourself you wouldn't.* However, something about her intrigued him. What?

"No time." His laptop dinged. His search brought nothing on Broderick. "No matches on the ring leader." He typed in Cash.

"I'm not surprised. Let's ask Gabe if he heard the names at either the cave or the ranch."

"Good idea. What if—"

A black SUV bolted onto the highway from a side road and rammed their bumper, spinning them around as freezing rain began pounding the windshield.

Hannah fought to maintain control of the Jeep. The tires hit a patch of ice and the vehicle careened toward oncoming traffic. She took her foot off the gas and kept the tires straight as she'd been taught but still couldn't gain control. She eased into the direction of the skid and held her breath, tension tightening her neck muscles. A moment later, she pulled the Jeep back to the right side. She stole a quick peek in the rearview mirror and noted the black SUV once again approached them at a crazy speed for the icy conditions. She prepared for impact but kept her eyes on the slippery highway. "Brace! They're coming back." She held the steering wheel in a tight grip and uttered a desperate prayer.

Layke spoke into his radio, requesting assistance and gave them their location.

But would someone make it in time to save them from the perpetrators? She pressed on the accelerator. They needed to outrun them, which, on these dangerous roads, would probably be impossible.

Her console lit up, announcing a call coming in through her Bluetooth. Unknown caller. She glanced at Layke.

"It may be about Gabe."

Right. She hit the Answer icon. "Morgan here."

"Give up the boy and we might let you live." The husky voice personified malicious plans.

"We have no intentions of doing that," Layke said. "We will find you."

"I wish you the best in making that happen. You've been warned. Now you and your families will pay." *Click.*

"How did they get your number?"

Sirens and flashing lights appeared in the distance. The cavalry was here. *Thank You, Lord.*

"No idea." She checked her rearview mirror. The SUV decreased its speed and did a U-turn. "They're retreating."

"They know they're surrounded. Did you notice the license plate?"

"No! I was too busy trying to keep the Jeep on the road." *Ouch.* Her tone came out a bit too harsh, but her heightened anxiety had bubbled to the surface with this recent attack. How did this gang know where they were constantly? "I'm sorry. I didn't mean to take my frustration out on you. My nerves are on edge."

He touched her arm. "It's okay. I understand. I didn't get the plate either. Pull over and let's talk to the constable."

She guided the Jeep to the edge of the highway and put her four-way hazards on. The cruiser pulled in behind them and the officer approached their vehicle. She turned off the ignition and hit the button to roll down her window.

The constable tipped his hat. It was a different officer than the ones they'd met earlier. He leaned on the window frame and glanced into the vehicle at eye level. "Good day. Are you both okay?"

Layke pulled out his badge and flashed it toward him. "I'm Constable Layke Jackson and this is border patrol officer Hannah Morgan. We're working together on a joint task force to apprehend a child-smuggling ring. We obviously are getting too close and they came after us. We didn't get the license plate number, but it was a black SUV."

The officer introduced himself. "Nice to meet you both. I heard about the task force, and our detachment is helping in whatever way we can."

Hannah smiled. "We appreciate that. This gang needs to be found before more kids are abducted."

"How can I help today?"

Layke pointed in the direction the SUV escaped. "They did a U-turn and went that way. Perhaps you can find them. We need to get back to one of the abducted boys we have in protective custody."

"I heard about Gabe. Where are you hiding him?"

Hannah glanced at Layke and bit her lip, hoping he'd catch her concern.

Layke gave a slight nod and returned his attention to the officer. "We're under strict guidelines to keep the location a secret. You understand. It's for the boy's protection."

And theirs.

The constable's expression contorted. "But we could help protect both you and the boy."

Clearly they had offended the willowy officer.

Hannah gripped the armrest. "We appreciate your good intentions, Constable. However, the boy is in danger and we can't risk that." Would he back down?

"Of course," the officer said, straightening and revealing his height. "I'll let you go and see if I can locate the SUV. I'll radio you if I find them. Stay safe." He patted the door frame.

"Will do." Layke pocketed his credentials.

She rolled the window back up and pulled away. "Thanks for catching my reaction to his question. My gut tells me we need to keep our location under the radar. Someone must be leaking information because who else knows where we are?"

"Agreed." His cell phone dinged and he glanced at the text. "Elias said the forensic artist is about forty-five minutes away from Murray's. That should put us both there around the same time."

"Perfect." She concentrated on the road conditions. The freezing rain had let up slightly, but the darkened clouds threatened more of the dangerous ice pellets.

Once Hannah reached Murray's ranch, the tension in her shoulders relaxed and her breathing returned to normal, although her chest was still heavy from the slam to the pavement she'd suffered after the blast. She pulled the Jeep into the driveway as a cruiser parked beside her. "Well, that was good timing."

Layke's eyes twinkled. "Great driving today."

Her breath hitched. She could get used to seeing those baby blues and that smile. It made her heart flutter uncontrollably. *Stop, Hannah. Remember what you have to offer. Nothing.* The word stuck in her throat like a fly to a sticky trap. It wouldn't let go. She forced a smile and opened her door. She had to somehow distance herself from this man and her growing feelings for him.

He climbed out of the Jeep and made his way over to the female constable. They shook hands and the woman glanced in Hannah's direction. The pretty raven-haired officer put her attention back on Layke and giggled at something he said, grabbing his arm. It was clear Layke's charm had wormed its way into the woman.

A pang stabbed Hannah's heart. How could she be jealous of someone she hadn't even met yet?

A text pinged and she pulled out her cell phone. Doyle. Leads on local fisheries came up empty. No trucks had been dispatched recently. She sighed. Another dead end. Really? How was that possible? Gabe was so sure of the fishy smell. *Odd.*

The front door opened and Gabe came running. He

threw his arms around her legs and squeezed. "I missed you, Miss Hannah."

Tears welled and she swallowed to keep the lump from forming. How would she ever be able to say goodbye to this precious child when this case was concluded? *God, what are You doing? Throwing a child at me after the news of my condition? You know my heart's desires.*

She rubbed the boy's arms. "Hey, bud. I missed you, too, but you need to put a coat on when you go outside. Let's get you back indoors." She glanced toward Layke to get his attention, but he was engrossed in a conversation with the constable.

Hannah ignored the ugly seed of jealousy creeping into her heart and guided Gabe up the stairs to the front door. "What did you do while we were gone?"

"I played with the dogs. They are so much fun." The boy's eyes lit up like a Christmas tree at a tree-lighting event. "I love Saje the best."

"The one with the different colored eyes?"

"Yes! She's so funny."

Hannah giggled. "I'll have to go visit the dogs later, but right now we have a lady here who needs to talk to you about the man you saw."

His smile faded as panic contorted his tiny face. "I can't." He opened the door and stomped into the entry-way, his wiry curls bouncing.

She followed him and removed her outerwear. "He can't hurt you here, Gabe. Mr. Layke and I won't let him."

"I don't want to talk to her." He ran into the living room.

Murray and Natalie walked around the corner.

"Is he okay?" Natalie asked, concern etched around her eyes.

"He's scared to speak to the forensic sketch artist."

"I'll go talk to him." Natalie walked into the room and sat on the couch beside Gabe, whispering something to him.

"She's good with kids," Hannah said.

Murray nodded. "She's always wanted to be a mother and we had a hard time conceiving, but God finally gave us Noel."

Would God do that for her? Was there hope?

Hannah brushed aside the trusting thought as the front door opened and Layke walked in with the pretty constable laughing.

Hannah bit her lip in an attempt to stop the green-eyed monster from overtaking her at the realization of how quickly the two constables had bonded.

Layke took off his coat. "Everyone, this is Constable Scarlet Wells. Scarlet, this is border patrol officer Hannah Morgan and my brother, Murray Harrelson."

Scarlet's lips tipped into a gorgeous smile.

No wonder Layke seemed smitten.

Hannah cleared her throat and thrust out her hand. "Nice to meet you. Gabe is in the living room, and very nervous about talking to you."

"Don't worry. I'll calm him. I'm great with kids." She took off her boots and picked up her briefcase before heading toward Gabe.

Of course you are.

Layke tilted his head at her, a searching expression on his face. "You okay?"

"Fine. Let's get this done." Her curt tone surprised even herself. Hannah had to stop this way of thinking. This jealousy wasn't an emotion she normally felt. She pivoted and left her words hanging in the air as she headed toward Gabe.

She had to keep her focus on him and the other boys. They needed to find them.

Before something terrible happened.

ELEVEN

Layke followed the crusty border patrol officer into the room. What had he done to cause her sudden shift in mood and why did he care so much? *You know why.* His feelings for Hannah had grown way too fast for his liking. Especially when he'd sworn himself off falling for any woman. He was resolved to remain single for the rest of his life, so why did he care about Hannah's coolness toward him?

Hannah sat on the other side of Gabe and rubbed the crying boy's arm as Scarlet talked to him about the process she would take.

Natalie stood behind them and squeezed Gabe's shoulders. "Bud, it's okay. You're safe here."

Three mother hens for one boy. He chuckled to himself as an image formed in his mind of birds clucking around a baby chick. This boy didn't stand a chance.

Scarlet drew out a tissue from her pocket and wiped his tears. "It's okay, Gabe. I will be quick because I'm good at what I do." She turned and smiled at Layke.

A pinched expression raced across Hannah's face, causing him to take a step back. Was she jealous of the pretty forensic artist? Why? Was it because of the attention Scarlet was giving the boy or the fact that Layke had hit it off quickly with the constable? They'd discovered they had mutual friends in their force and shared a couple quick stories with each other that made him laugh.

No, it couldn't be that. Hannah wasn't interested in Layke anyway. Was she?

Stop. Concentrate. Remember what Amber did to you. He sat in the rocking chair beside them. "Sport, it's okay. You can talk to Miss Scarlet. She's only here to help. You need to tell her what the bad man looks like."

Hannah cleared her throat and raised her brow at him.

What had he done wrong?

Scarlet pulled out a coiled notebook from her briefcase. "First, I'm going to show you some images of faces to help jog your memory. Okay?"

Gabe frowned.

She held the book in front of him. "Did the man look like any of these?"

He shook his head.

"How about these ones?" She turned the page.

"Nope."

She flipped to another and held it up.

He shook his head and crossed his arms.

The boy's body language personified annoyance. Layke had to intervene.

"Sport, I know you're scared and don't want to do this, but it will help us catch the bad guys. Can you cooperate?"

Once again, Hannah cleared her throat.

He looked at her. "What?"

She stood. "Can I speak with you in private for a minute?" She marched into the kitchen.

He followed. "What's wrong with you?"

She spun around, her eyes narrowing. "You have to stop forcing him. He's young and scared."

He sighed. "Hannah, we need to find Noel and the other boys, but first we need to identify this man."

"Stop being so pushy."

He leaned against the counter and crossed his arms. "What's really going on here? Your mood shifted after Scarlet came."

She looked away but not before he caught her flattened lips. "I'm fine."

"Why are you annoyed with me? Did I do something wrong?"

"I don't like you pressuring him. He's fragile." She twiddled with her belt.

"Hannah, I know body language. There's something you're not saying." He stepped toward her. "Tell me."

"You just seem so cozy with Scarlet." She clamped her hand over her mouth, indicating she hadn't meant to utter the words.

She *was* jealous. "Hannah, when we introduced ourselves, we realized we knew some of the same people."

"But you were laughing a lot with her. You don't laugh much normally."

He didn't? When had he become so rigid? He thought he'd had it under control, but Amber's recent betrayal had sucked the joy from his life. Would he ever learn to trust again?

Layke took Hannah's hands in hers. "I'm sorry. She was telling me a funny story about a coworker." He paused. "That's all it was."

I'm not interested in the forensic artist. It's you who's capturing my heart.

Their gaze locked as he held her hands.

"Um, excuse me," Scarlet said.

Layke dropped Hannah's hands as disappointment crossed her face. "What is it?"

"Gabe is chatting nonstop now. We're close to a sketch." The irritation in her blunt tone filled the room as she spun on her heels and walked back into the living room.

What was going on here?

Hannah smirked at him.

"What?"

"Seems like you've annoyed the pretty constable."

Was that satisfaction on her face?

He couldn't win.

He shook his head and moved back into the living room. The roaring fire filled the rustic room, creating a cozy mood. He only hoped it helped calm the tension. He sat beside Gabe. "Hey, sport, what else do you remember?"

"The bad man had spiky hair."

"You told us that earlier. What else?"

Gabe pointed at the page. "His eyes look like that."

The sketch of a man with narrow eyes far apart appeared on the page.

Scarlet switched to one with various nose types. "What about his nose?"

Gabe pointed to a wide, flat one.

"That's so good, Gabe. What about his chin?"

Scarlet flipped to show him examples.

"He has ears like you, Mr. Layke."

Layke fingered his ears. What was wrong with them?

Scarlet giggled and picked up her pencil. "That's excellent, Gabe. I will start drawing and you can tell me if it's right, okay?"

The boy nodded.

"Gabe, do you remember hearing the name 'Cash' either at the cave or the ranch?" Layke asked.

"No." The boy slouched back in the chair.

Hannah stood beside the couch. "Can he take a break?"

Scarlet eyed the border patrol officer, her steady gaze clearly sizing her up. "Fine. I won't be long though. I'll go to the dining room to sketch. I need quietness to compose." She left the room.

Hannah held out her hand to Gabe. "Bud, let's go find

something to eat. It's past lunchtime. You must be hungry. That okay, Natalie?"

The woman hopped up. "Of course. I'll show you what we have."

Hannah and Gabe followed her into the kitchen.

Murray sat in the corner, his hands holding his head.

Layke clenched his jaw. They needed to find Noel before it was too late. He walked over to his half brother and placed his hand on his burly shoulder. "You okay?"

Murray looked up at him. "I was praying for God to find Noel."

Layke fidgeted with the button on his plaid shirt and studied the hardwood floor.

"You don't believe?"

He sighed and glanced back at Murray's face. "I'm sorry. I don't." Even though he'd felt His presence earlier, he still wasn't ready to surrender.

"You don't have to apologize. Can I ask you a question?"

"Sure," Layke sat in the matching plaid wing chair beside Murray.

"Dad told me you came to see him this past summer, but he wouldn't talk to you. Do you know why?"

"No idea. Are you in contact with him?"

"He writes me letters. He told me he was scared to let you come to the prison."

"Why?"

"Remorse. That's why he refused your visit."

What? Not the words he expected to hear. "What do you mean?"

"Even though our father did what he did, he still loves his family. He couldn't face you, knowing you were a cop."

Layke fingered the button on his plaid shirt. This was a side of his father he had never expected to hear about.

A side that shocked him to the bone. "Tell me more. What was it like growing up with him?"

"Interesting. Never a dull moment."

"What do you mean?" Layke asked.

"He was away a lot with his job, but it increased after I turned ten. Then we would find him in the basement studying anatomy textbooks."

"Why?"

"He became fascinated with the human body."

"Is that when our father began murdering?"

A crash sounded behind him.

Hannah stood with a sandwich plate broken at her feet.

Great. Now he'd have to explain his past.

After he swore to himself he'd never let anyone know his family's dark secret.

Hannah squatted and began cleaning up the mess she'd made. Had she heard Layke correctly? His father was a murderer? It couldn't be. Was that why he got into policing? A million questions raced through her mind as she picked up the broken plate and tuna sandwiches. What if—

Layke knelt beside her and placed his hand over top of her shaky one. "I'm not like him, Hannah."

She couldn't explain the sudden anxiousness stirring inside her. Flashes of angry men living on the streets with her and Kaylin after she'd ran away from an abusive foster home popped into her head.

"I'll get a broom," Murray said.

She continued to wipe off the sandwiches, trying to hide her frayed nerves. *Get a grip on yourself.*

"Stop." Layke squeezed her hand and pulled her to her feet, holding her at the waist. "I'm sorry you heard that. I wasn't quite ready to share it with anyone yet."

She stared into his eyes and tried to read them for any sign of deceit. Only kindness shone on his face, and she chastised herself for even thinking he could be violent. "I'm sorry for making a mess on the floor." Her voice sounded weak.

"I'm sure they have other plates." He brushed a curl from her face. "Hannah, I'll tell you about Henry Harrelson another time. I don't want to talk about him yet."

"It's okay. I understand. You don't need to give me an explanation." After all, once this case was over, he'd be out of her life anyway. The thought of his absence brought an inexplicable ache in her heart. How was that even possible? She couldn't fall for anyone with the burden she carried. She'd barely had time to process the fact that she couldn't have children. Plus, they'd just met. Could intense attraction explode that quickly?

Murray walked into the room with the broom and garbage can. "Coming through."

Hannah stepped back to allow Murray between them. It was for the best. She needed to stay away from Layke's touch. It kept doing strange things to her feelings, and she knew she had to curb them—fast.

Scarlet returned, waving her sketch with Gabe at her side. "We got it. Gabe agreed this is the man at the ranch."

Hannah and Layke peered at her composite. A man with spiked hair snarled back at them.

Hannah froze.

Layke grabbed her arm. "What is it?"

"That's the man from the border crossing. The one who saw my face."

And was probably after her because she could recognize him. If she didn't say it out loud maybe it wouldn't be true. Hardly. Reality sank in. Her life was also in jeopardy.

Layke stood in front of her. "We will catch him. I won't let him hurt you." His voice held a gentleness to it.

Her heart danced a beat.

"I'll send it in so we can put it through facial recognition." Scarlet grabbed her equipment and went back to the dining room.

"Hopefully, we'll get a match." Layke walked back over to Murray and lifted the garbage can so his brother could dump the ruined porcelain-laced sandwiches into it.

Layke's cell phone buzzed and he pulled it from his jean's pocket. "Just got a text from Elias saying they got a hit on the license plate from the truck. With the partial number, make and model of the truck, they were able to determine it belongs to a Tupper Cash."

"Cash! The name Rob gave us. Broderick's right-hand man."

They were getting closer.

"We got an address." Layke angled his phone at Murray. "You know this place?"

Murray's eyes widened. "It's a few kilometers into Alaska."

"How long will it take us to get there?"

Murray looked outside. "About seventy-five minutes in good weather. The freezing rain is starting again, so you should wait until it lets up."

"We can't. We need to catch this guy. He could be the key to finding Noel."

Murray placed his hand on Layke's shoulder. "Brother, we just found each other. I don't want to lose you, too."

Layke's face softened. "I know, but I want to find Noel." They embraced.

Hannah's eyes moistened at their exchange. The emerging bond between the brothers was evident.

Murray pulled back. "Okay, if you're going then you will need an emergency winter travel kit." He left the room.

Hannah pulled the keys from her pocket. "You're driving this time."

Scarlet rushed back into the room. "That's the fastest result I've ever had. We've identified the man."

Layke glanced at Hannah. "Let me guess. Tupper Cash?"

Scarlet frowned. "How did you know?"

"Just got a hit on his truck. We're headed now to his address in Alaska."

"You and her? Is she trained?" Scarlet pointed to Hannah, the disdain heavy in her tone.

Hannah stiffened. When would people realize CBSA officers were trained on more than interview and communication skills? She excelled in her defensive and firearms classes.

"Hannah knows what she's doing. I've seen evidence of it." Layke grabbed his jacket from the chair he'd thrown it on earlier. "We gotta roll."

"Should I stay with Gabe?" Scarlet fingered the weapon at her side. "We can't leave him alone with civilians without protection."

"No one but us knows he's here, Scarlet." Hannah bit her lip, silencing what she really wanted to say to the pushy officer.

Scarlet grabbed at Layke's arm, ignoring Hannah's comment. "Layke, I think I should stay. I brought an overnight bag with me and the roads are iffy. There must be an extra room in this enormous house."

Really? This woman had an obvious crush on the handsome constable.

"I'll check with Murray on the way out, but I'm sure it would be fine." He turned to Hannah. "We should probably have someone else here protecting Gabe. This case is too unpredictable to take any further chances."

She sighed, knowing he was right. Gabe needed protection.

Even if it meant the irritating woman had to stay.

Eighty minutes later, Layke pulled into the parking lot of the apartment building in Alaska housing the parolee

Tupper Cash. Now that they had a composite sketch, Layke had Corporal Bakker put a BOLO out on Cash in Canada and with the US authorities in Alaska. He'd also requested a state trooper meet them at Tupper's apartment. Hannah had used Layke's laptop to find out more about Cash and read the information to him on the drive into the States. Forty-two years old, born in Anchorage, Alaska, served time in a US prison for armed robbery, assault and human trafficking. What drove a person to commit these crimes? A question he'd struggled with ever since he became a cop and even more so when he found out about his father.

Hannah updated her boss on the situation, and they were now waiting for a possible lead on a scheduled smuggling drop happening soon. Superintendent Walsh was in contact with an informant and would let them know more once he heard back.

Layke was hopeful Cash could lead them to the ring. They only had to catch him and convince him to talk. That would be the challenge. Layke was hopeful a US district attorney would give Cash a plea in exchange for securing the children. Maybe.

Thankfully, the freezing rain had subsided and their uneventful drive over to Alaska was a welcome change, for which Hannah had given praise to God out loud. Could he put his trust in a God who had abandoned him? Even after this morning? He wasn't sure, but the witness of Hannah, Murray and Natalie impressed him. They'd shown intense faith in difficult circumstances. Deep down, he wanted that same faith. If only he wasn't so skeptical. Why couldn't he take that leap and step into the unknown and unseen? He pushed the poignant question aside. He'd give it more thought later.

He parked the Jeep beside a dented Ford 150. "I think this is Cash's truck. We're in the right place. Stay alert."

"Always." She climbed from the Jeep.

He followed and checked the truck's license plate. "It's a match, and it appears that our suspect is home. For once, we're one step ahead of them. Let's go, and stay behind me."

"Will do."

He peered at the three-story walk-up. The dilapidated building needed urgent care. He noted shingles missing, broken balcony railings and the front door hanging from its hinges.

"This building doesn't look safe. Be careful." Layke took a step as an SUV pulled out of its parking spot only just missing him. "Watch out!" He shoved her to the side, pushing her from harm's way.

The vehicle raced out of the parking lot like a race car driver. Someone definitely on a mission. Wait—

"Did that SUV look like the one trying to run us off the road earlier?" It came so quickly he'd missed the license plate.

"It was dark like the previous one."

Not good.

"Let's get to Cash's apartment." Something told him he wouldn't like what he found.

A state trooper walked toward them and extended his hand. "Officer Jim Allard. I've been apprised of the situation."

Layke made introductions and they entered the building, taking the stairs cautiously. He didn't trust anything about the structure. He checked the numbers posted on the wall to determine which direction to head, then turned right. Layke halted. He immediately noticed Cash's broken door. He unleashed his weapon and turned to Hannah. "This doesn't look good. Be prepared for anything."

She pulled out her gun but stayed behind him.

"Officer, this is your jurisdiction," Layke said. "You lead."

The trooper edged the door open and stepped inside. "Police! Identify yourself."

Silence and musty air greeted them.

Layke walked into the living room with Hannah at his heels.

She gasped.

He turned to see her gaze focused on the couch.

A foot protruded from behind it.

Layke rushed over to investigate and braced himself for what he'd find.

Tupper Cash lay on the floor with a bullet in his head, his lifeless eyes staring at the ceiling.

TWELVE

Hannah listened as Layke spoke to Goliath-type Alaska state trooper Jim Allard. She sighed. Their first real hope of solving this case had been taken out with a single shot. The image of the dark SUV barreling out of the parking lot now made sense. They had just missed the assassination. Could they have stopped it? Had the gang discovered they were on their way to interrogate Tupper and decided to take him out? He obviously knew too much.

"This guy has been on our radar," Jim said. "However, we haven't been able to catch him in any act of crime."

"What can you tell us about him?" Layke had his pen and notebook ready.

"Cash is known in these parts as a major troublemaker. Always involved in the next get-rich-quick scheme, no matter the cost." He knelt beside the body. "Looks like this was an assassination. Didn't stand any hopes of survival."

Hannah stepped closer. She'd seen a few bodies, but none taken out like Tupper. Nausea slammed her and she gagged. She covered her mouth and turned away from the pair. She wouldn't let them see the effect this body had on her. *Breathe, Hannah, breathe.* She inhaled deeply through her nose and exhaled through her mouth. She pulled out her inhaler and took a puff.

Layke touched her back. "Hannah, you okay?"

Busted.

His gentle hand at the small of her back somehow eased the terror threatening to consume her body. She could get used to him by her side. She shoved the thought away and turned. "I'm fine. Just hit me wrong."

A knock at the door sounded.

Jim jumped up. "That would be the crime scene investigator." He let in the lanky young man.

Layke's eyes widened and he leaned closer. "Looks like a teenager," he whispered.

His minty breath tickled her ear and she shivered. "I know, right?" Her cell phone played Doyle's ring. She fished it out of her pocket. "What do you have for me, boss man."

"I hate when you call me that."

"I know." She chuckled.

"Listen, my contact got back to me. Seems like there's a smuggling drop happening at midnight tonight." He continued to tell her about the airstrip where the plane was expected to land. She tilted her head and cradled the phone between her chin and shoulder, grabbing Layke's notebook and pen. "Give that to me again." She jotted the information down. "Got it. We'll be there. Will you?"

"No, I'm following another lead. Can you and Constable Jackson handle it along with the other border patrol officers?"

"We'll be fine. Give me the contact's info in case we need to call him." She added it to her scribbles in Layke's notebook. "Got it."

"Be safe, little one."

She smiled at his term of endearment. "Always." She clicked off.

"What's happening?"

Hannah told him about the smuggling drop. She checked her watch. The day had gotten away from them and it would soon be dusk. "We need to leave if we're going to get there on time. How about we grab some munchies for the stakeout?" Excitement bubbled and she bounced in place.

"Have you ever been on a stakeout?"

"No. Why?"

"They're not as fun as television portrays them. Boring, actually."

She never believed anything she saw on the tube. They rarely got their facts straight. "Can we head out now?"

"I'll check." He conversed with Trooper Allard and they agreed to stay in touch. Sharing information between the two agencies was necessary in this case. Layke pulled the keys out, dangling them. "Let's go."

Thirty minutes later, Hannah directed Layke back across the quiet border crossing and into Canada. The freezing rain had returned with a vengeance. A thick layer of ice covered the trees, fields and hydro lines. She sent up a quick prayer for their safety. The Yukon roads in the winter were already tricky enough, and throwing in a layer of ice only added to the danger. To think her life forty-eight hours ago was quiet and boring. She studied Layke's handsome profile. God definitely had a sense of humor. With the news of her condition of polycystic ovary syndrome, He throws a man in her path she could fall for and see herself with years from now? Who was she kidding? She was already on her way to doing just that. Was God teasing her? She couldn't fall for a potential husband when she would never be able to give him a child.

Trust.

The word raced through her mind like God had whispered it in her ear. How could she trust Him when her life was crumbling? She turned her head and stared at the passing icy trees, pressing her lips tightly together. No, God had failed her. She'd poured out her heart to Him, confessing her heart's desire. However, He hadn't listened.

Why, God? Haven't I followed You all these years? Done Your work?

She sighed. A little too loudly.

"What's wrong?" Layke asked.

He'd be horrified if he could read her thoughts. How could she share her doubts about God's sovereign plan and her identity in Him when Layke couldn't trust God for reasons she didn't know? She needed this case to be over so she could go off by herself and mourn the loss of not being able to have children. "Nothing. Just wishing we could solve this case."

He shifted his gaze toward her. "Are you sure that's all?"

Man, he needed to stop getting into her head. "I'm sure."

At that moment, the car slid to the left and the tires locked in a skid.

"Watch out!" She pointed to an oncoming car. She gripped the armrest as if it were her lifeline.

Layke took his foot off the gas, but she could feel him losing control of the car on the sheet of ice.

She held her breath as the vehicle inched closer to them almost like it was in slow motion. It veered right, then left.

Then lurched into their path at full speed.

"Hold on!" Layke fought for control.

Hannah shut her eyes and waited for impact.

Layke's defensive driving training kicked into gear and he turned the wheel to the right to get out of the car's trajectory. He uttered a prayer that the tires would find traction and stay on the icy highway. This was exactly why he hated winter and could never live in a place where the season held its victims in a polar grip for too many months. Calgary was wintery enough for him.

Miraculously, the Jeep remained on course and Layke

regained control. The oncoming car swerved around them and out of harm's way.

Hannah let out a staggered sigh. "Praise the Lord."

For once he couldn't argue with her statement. Had God really heard his desperate plea for safety? "Well, that was fun. Not." He relaxed his fierce hold on the wheel and stole a peek at the pretty border patrol officer.

She still held the armrest like it was her saving grace. She tightened her lips as a red curl fell in front of her eye. She huffed out a breath to remove it from her face, but it didn't work.

Did she realize how cute she was, especially when she didn't know she was being watched?

He returned his gaze to the highway. A sudden wave of emotion washed over him like a waterfall on a warm summer day. Was his heart opening a crack to allow a woman into his life? This woman? At this moment, he wanted nothing more than to take her into his arms and protect her from every danger in her path.

An image of Amber's face flashed before him as he kept his eyes on the stormy road. She had played him when he thought she was interested and damaged his trust in women. He'd almost lost his job over her shenanigans. Layke clenched his jaw as the vein in his neck pulsed, closing shut the crack in his heart. No, he wouldn't let a woman into his life. Besides, after this case he would be going back to Calgary and he would not do a long-distance relationship. Even if he wanted one. Which he didn't. He made a promise to himself that he would spend his life free of romantic relationships.

"What are you thinking?" Hannah asked.

"How much I hate winter." A half-truth.

"It's my favorite time of year. Well, ice storms are too dangerous for my liking."

His cell phone rang, jarring him from their conversation. He hit the speaker button. "Constable Jackson here."

"Hello…" The timid voice could barely be heard through the car's Bluetooth.

"Who's this?"

"Don Crawford. You called about my son?"

Right, the final parent he needed to talk to from the list Murray gave him. "Thank you for returning my call, Mr. Crawford. You're on speakerphone and I have border patrol officer Hannah Morgan with me. What can you tell us about the day your son was kidnapped?"

The man cleared his voice. "Not much. My wife dropped him off at the church, and a day later we received a call from the police that he was missing along with the other boys."

His nonchalant tone piqued Layke's interest. No quiver and his previously timid voice had disappeared. Odd. "Were you ever contacted for a ransom demand?" None of the other parents had been, but he needed to ask anyway.

Silence.

Layke glanced at Hannah.

She steeled her jaw.

Her inquisitive look revealed she had the same suspicions about this man.

He made a mental note to check the system for any prior arrests. "Mr. Crawford? You still there?"

"Yes. I don't know anything and I have to go."

"Call us if you think—"

Click.

Hannah pushed the button to end the call. "Okay, that was weird. His silence tells me he's hiding something. But what?"

"Grab my laptop. I'm already logged into our database. Can you search for his name?"

"You think he might be involved?"

"Not saying that, but I need to be sure."

She snatched the device from the back seat, opened it and started typing.

They waited.

A ding sounded on his laptop. "What does it say?"

"Oh, my. Donald E. Crawford. Arrested five years ago for assault with a deadly weapon and kidnapping of a child."

Bingo.

"What else?"

"Lawyer got him off on a technicality. Acquitted of all charges after his wife testified on his behalf. Says here she provided an alibi for the date in question."

Layke swerved around a fallen branch. "What happened to the child who was kidnapped?"

She glanced back to the screen. "Says here the child was never found and no one was convicted. That poor family." She closed the laptop. "Wait! I remember that case. I had just moved here. It was all over the news."

"What happened?"

"The child's mother committed suicide a year later. Her agony over the loss of her child was too much for her. Her husband moved away."

He clenched his jaw. He hated to hear heartbreaking news like that. Where was God in this situation?

"Do you really think Mr. Crawford would kidnap his own son?" Hannah asked.

"I hope not, but interesting he was charged for it in a prior case. We need to look into him further."

His stomach growled. He glanced at the time on the dashboard. No wonder. They hadn't eaten in hours. "Change of subject. Is there a coffee shop where we can grab some java and a muffin or something? We still have time before the scheduled drop."

"There's a coffee shop not far from here. Take your next right."

Ten minutes later, they waited in the long drive-through line. "Is it always this busy?"

"Yup. It's known for their amazing coffee beans and apple fritters. Trust me?"

Did he? He barely knew her, but something deep in his soul wanted to.

The beautiful redhead's smile enticed him. And those eyes...

Well, they lured him in and he could get lost in their ocean of blue.

He cleared his foggy mind from her magnetic embrace. *Remember the last redhead you let into your life.* "Sure." Really, what did he have to lose? Other than his heart.

He let out a long breath and rested his head as they waited in the line. His shoulders lowered as he felt himself relax for the first time in forty-eight hours.

"Good, you're relaxing."

Was it that obvious? "I've been so wound lately."

"You mean before coming to the Yukon? Why?"

He stared into her eyes, trying to decide whether or not he could trust her with his secret.

She placed her hand over his. "You can trust me and I don't bite."

Wow. She *was* good at her job of reading people. But could he really share something he hadn't even told his best friend, Hudson? Even though they'd only met, they had been thrust into a perilous situation. People got close fast when danger happened.

No, he wasn't ready. He pulled his hand away.

Disappointment shone in her expression, kicking him in the gut. He hadn't meant to hurt her. "It's a long story. Sorry."

"And we just met. I get it."

He pulled out his cell phone. "Let's call and check on Gabe. It's probably time for him to go to bed." Besides, he had to change the subject. He punched in Murray's number, put it on speaker and set it on the console in the middle of the Jeep. His half brother answered on the second ring.

"Hey, man. How's everything going there with Gabe?"

"Great. We're sitting on his bed reading him a story right now."

"Mr. Layke, is that you?" Gabe's cheerful voice sailed through the cell phone.

"Yes. I'm here with Miss Hannah. We wanted to say good-night."

"I miss you. When are you coming back?"

"Soon, sport." He hoped.

"We'll help you build a snowman tomorrow," Hannah said. "Sound good?"

"Yay! I wanna hear the end of your story, Mr. Layke. Please."

He smirked. "Sure. Where was I?"

"The knight killed the dragon."

"Right." Layke paused, pondering an ending for his tale. "Marian ran from her hiding place and hugged Richard. 'You saved me,' she said." Layke once again changed his voice into a woman's. "Richard helped Marian onto Shadowfax and galloped back to the kingdom."

"Did she marry him or did that mean Knight Arthur steal her?" Gabe asked.

"I was getting to that part," Layke said. "She confessed her hidden love for Richard and asked her father to let them marry."

"Yes!" Gabe yelled.

"They lived happily ever after like all the fairy tales."

Hannah drummed on the dashboard. "Well, did they kiss?"

Layke's face flushed. Why did the simple question embarrass him? Was it because the thought of kissing Hannah captured his attention? He stared at her pink lips.

She cleared her throat and looked down, fumbling with her parka zipper.

"Well?" Gabe's excited voice brought him back to story land.

"Of course they did. Richard pulled Marian into a long hug and kissed her. The end."

Clapping, along with Murray's laughter, exploded through the cell phone. "Time for bed, Gabe. Say good-night to Hannah and Layke."

"Night, Mr. Layke. Thanks for the story. Night, Miss Hannah. I love you."

A saddened expression flitted across her face so fast he almost missed it. What about Gabe's affections grieved her?

Her lips curved into a smile. "Love you, too. Night, bud. Sweet dreams."

Her tone conveyed a mother's love. Layke flinched. His growing feelings for this woman had to be squelched. He could never give a wife a child. Not after his painful childhood. He would not take that chance.

Layke, you're not your mother.

He raked his fingers through his hair as he fought with himself. He'd gone for counseling to get rid of the anger from his past, but sometimes it consumed his thoughts. He vowed to never let it get the best of him. So far, he had succeeded.

"Night. I want you to be my mommy," Gabe whispered.

Hannah pressed her eyes shut but not before he caught them moisten. Grief once again etched lines on her face. Something about this boy brought her sadness. What?

"Stay safe. See you when you get back," Murray said.

"You got it." Layke hung up and reached for Hannah's hand. "You okay?"

"I'm—" Her cell phone jingled. "Doyle, what's up?" A pause.

She straightened in her seat. "We're on our way." She stuffed her phone into her pocket. "The meet has been moved up and the location changed. The plane can't land in the snowstorm. It's happening in thirty minutes, and we still have to get there in this weather."

"Let's go." He pulled out from the lineup and back onto the highway. So much for a bite to eat. Coffee would have to wait until another time.

They had a smuggling ring to catch.

Hannah gripped the armrest once again as Layke sped down the highway. The temperature had plummeted, turning the icy conditions into a full-blown snowstorm, which she'd take over freezing rain anytime. However, they had to get to the drop site quickly and the weather wasn't helping.

Gabe's earlier comment about him wanting her to be his mother tore at her soul. Every inch of her longed for motherhood. *God, what are You doing?*

Plus, the fact that Layke had managed to tug at her heartstrings even though he'd pulled away from her earlier. What was his story? She was curious to find out. Why?

You know why. She'd begun to fall for this rugged, handsome man. *You can't, Hannah. Remember your secret.* He was clearly good with children and she could never give him one. That was even if he was interested. Which he obviously wasn't.

Ugh! She pounded the armrest.

"What's wrong?"

Oops. Contain your feelings. "Nothing. Just frustrated with this weather." Well, sort of true.

"How did your boss know the change of plans?"

"His informant." She peered out the window at the darkness. The headlights revealed the heavy snow impeding their path. She glanced at her watch. "We need to get there or we'll miss them."

"I'm driving as fast as I can in this."

"There!" She pointed to a side road. "Turn right. We're almost there."

The Jeep fishtailed with the hard shift in direction. Layke fought to keep it on the road and managed to straighten. They continued until they reached a small crossing.

A border patrol car was parked under secluded trees.

"Park there. That's my fellow border officers. They're here to help."

Layke pulled in behind the cruiser. "Good. We can use their assistance." He grasped his radio and conveyed their location. "Local authorities are en route, as well."

"Good." She exited the Jeep and knocked on the cruiser's window. "Can we join you?"

The officer unlocked the doors and they climbed in the back.

"Hey, guys. Nice to see you again," Hannah said. "Officers Shields and Walker, this is Constable Layke Jackson on loan to us from Calgary."

"Good to see you again, Officer Morgan," Officer Shields said, and extended his hand. "Constable, nice to meet you."

"Is this a normal border crossing?" Layke asked.

"No, it's a back way into Canada and rarely used." Officer Walker tugged on his tuque, exposing his blond hair. "Sometimes we catch drug dealers smuggling through this route."

"Why not shut it down?"

"We've tried everything to do just that, but it's been unsuccessful." Officer Shields took a drink from his mug.

Hannah eyed the chips in the front. "Can we have some? We had to abandon our snack run to get here."

He tossed the bag to them. "Help yourselves."

Layke scrunched his nose. "Not a healthy supper."

Hannah stuffed some chips in her mouth and mumbled, "Don't care."

The cruiser's radio crackled. "My informant should be there any moment," Superintendent Doyle said. "Stay alert and don't trust anyone. Not even him."

A headlight peered through an opening in the trees. A snowmobile raced across the field toward them. Its engine grew louder and sliced into the silent night.

Layke pulled out his weapon.

The radio crackled again. "He's arriving on a snow-mobile."

Hannah put her hand on Layke's. "Stay cool. That's Doyle's informant." She knew what he was thinking. The assailants from yesterday had been on a snowmobile. She opened the door and stepped out into the polar vortex evening. The snow pelted her face, stinging her cheeks. She pulled her hat down farther on her head and fastened her parka's zipper tighter at her neck.

The officers and Layke stood beside her as the snow-mobile pulled up and a spindly man climbed off.

"Does everyone ride one of those?" Layke asked.

"Almost. Although, Murray rides a sled." Hannah tugged at her insulated gloves, shoving them higher up her wrists. Any exposed skin in this weather would suffer quickly.

"We should take one out when we get back. Give the dogs a workout."

Had Layke just admitted to wanting to take in a winter activity? She tilted her head.

"Don't be so surprised," he said. "I'm getting used to this place."

She loved the idea of going on a sled ride with him but

put her concentration back on the man approaching. She stuck out her hand. "Officer Morgan here. You are?"

"My name doesn't matter. Doyle sent me. The package is arriving at any minute."

Layke stepped forward. "The package? You mean innocent lives." He latched on to the informant's arm. "How do you know about it? Are you involved?" He squeezed harder.

The man yelped.

Hannah shone her light at him.

His eyes bulged. "No! I have someone on the inside."

Officer Shields pulled Layke off the informant. "Take it easy, Constable. We're all on the same side here."

"We are?" Layke's tone conveyed his frustration.

They had to find his nephew before Layke lost it.

Hannah held up her hands in a stop position. "Take it easy, everyone. Sir, can you tell us who's the head of this ring?"

He shook his head. "I've only heard a name. Broderick. He has high connections."

Him again. Who was this mysterious person, and what connections? "Where can we find this gang? We know they're keeping the boys at a ranch somewhere in the area."

"Nope. It's well hidden. Not even some of his men know."

Officer Walker pulled out a notepad. "Can you give us names of these men?"

The man huffed. "And get myself killed? No way, man. Besides, I only knew of one—Tupper—and he's dead."

"How do you know that?" Layke asked.

"It's called the dark web, Constable. You'd be surprised what you can find out there."

Layke rubbed his forehead. "Watch your attitude or we'll arrest you for aiding and abetting."

Once again the man's eyes bulged. "You can't do that."

"You'd—"

Multiple engines sounded through the darkness.

They fell silent.

Lights appeared along the tree line. Snowmobiles approached at high speed.

Layke pulled out his weapon. "Take cover!"

Shots pummeled the area and pierced the night.

Hannah's shoulder stung and she fell backward, stumbling over fallen branches. The arctic snow-covered ground swallowed her up, threatening to encompass her entire body. She clasped her hand on the wound as nausea struck and her consciousness blurred.

"Hannah!"

Somewhere in the distance she heard Layke's muffled voice.

Darkness called out to her, but she fought it.

Until the pain wrenched her into its clutches and entwined her with murky blackness.

THIRTEEN

Layke raced to Hannah's side and scrambled to pull her behind the Jeep and out of the assailants' reach. Where had they come from and who'd ordered the hit? Was it the dark web again? The spindly informant hustled away on his snowmobile before they could question him further, but Layke couldn't concern himself with the man. Hannah had been shot, and the crimson snow around her proved she was losing blood fast.

The snowmobiles approached again, getting ready for another pass. The masked men aimed their machine guns.

Layke raised his weapon and pulled the trigger, firing multiple shots.

The CBSA officers discharged their Berettas, providing additional protection.

The snowmobiles retreated into the woods.

"Hannah!" Layke stuffed his weapon into its holster and knelt beside her, placing his hands on her wound. He turned to Officer Shields. "Where is the nearest medical facility?" He couldn't wait for the local authorities to arrive.

"The hospital is an hour away."

"She'll bleed out by then!" Layke couldn't lose her this way. She'd become too important to him even though he wouldn't admit that out loud. *God, save her!*

Officer Walker stumbled over. "Wait, there's a medical clinic just over the border in Alaska. We can use the same route as the smugglers."

Layke stood and pulled her into his arms. "I'll take her in the Jeep. You lead the way. Officer Shields, can you contain the situation here when the local authorities arrive? They should be here soon."

He nodded and walked over to his vehicle.

Fifteen minutes later, Layke followed the flashing CBSA cruiser into the Alaskan clinic's parking lot.

A nurse rushed out the front doors as Layke jumped out and lifted Hannah into his arms.

"What happened?" the petite nurse asked.

"She's been shot in the shoulder. I'm Canadian police constable Layke Jackson. We didn't have time to get her to a Canadian hospital."

Officer Walker ran to join them. "She's one of us. A border patrol officer. Can you help?"

"Our clinic is small but capable." She held the doors.

A plump doctor approached them. "I'm Dr. Hobbs. What happened?"

"She took a shot to the shoulder twenty minutes ago," Layke said. "She's lost blood."

Dr. Hobbs pushed his round-rimmed glasses farther up his nose and opened a door. "Bring her in here." He turned to the nurse. "Suit up. I need your help in the examination."

Two hours later, Layke paced the small waiting room. What was taking so long? The border patrol officer called in the situation and left to go back to Canada while Layke waited at the small clinic. He called Murray and told him what had happened. They promised to pray.

Pray? Once again, God had let him down. Why did He even let this happen in the first place? Not only had He allowed those boys to be taken, but now Hannah's life was in jeopardy. He shifted his gaze upward. *Why? Are You even there?*

The doors opened, interrupting Layke's thoughts.

Dr. Hobbs pulled down his mask and approached. "She was fortunate. The bullet grazed her shoulder and didn't hit any vital arteries. Someone up there was looking out after her."

Could it be true? God had saved her? Like He had Layke?

Layke let out the breath he felt he'd been holding for the past two hours. "Thank you, Doctor. Can I see her?"

The front door opened and another patient entered. He was holding his stomach and was followed by a young man in a ball cap. The twentysomething-year-old brushed the snow from his jacket and kept his head dipped.

"I gotta get back to work. She's still sedated but, yes, you can wait in the room." He left to attend to the other patients.

Layke walked through the doors and into the room.

Hannah's ashen face appeared out from behind the white sheets as the machine beeped a steady heartbeat.

Thank God.

Had he just thanked the One he'd been battling with earlier?

Layke sighed and pulled up a chair beside Hannah's bed. He didn't understand God. Why did He save some and not others? A question Layke would never be able to figure out. It seemed God didn't follow rules, and rules were what Layke lived by.

But why? Were they worth it?

He ignored the struggle going on inside him and held Hannah's cold hand. "Come on. Come back to me, sweet Hannah."

His cell phone buzzed. He glanced at the screen. Elias. "Hey, what's up?"

"How is she?"

"You heard?"

"Yes, Scarlet called after you let Murray know. Any news?"

"The bullet only grazed her, thankfully. She's recovering but not awake yet." He rubbed her hand, trying to warm it up.

"We need to talk."

The corporal's serious tone told Layke to give him his undivided attention. He got up and stepped out the door. "Okay. What's going on?" He walked down the hall to the back of the clinic and peered outside. The storm still hadn't let up.

"Couple things. We heard back from the constables at the scene of the medical center. Slug was from a 9 mm, so not helpful. But we got a hit on your victim Rob. His brother is bad news."

"His brother?"

"Yes, a politician in the Northwest Territories that's linked to the mafia. Have you heard of the Martells?"

Layke's stomach lurched. "As in Perry Martell? Yes, he's known across Canada and has evaded capture for years. No one can prove the politician is dirty. Why?"

"Rob was his brother and we're now on the Martell radar."

Layke sank against the wall. "What?"

"Watch your back. Our informants are telling us they've crossed into Yukon Territory and are out for revenge. Plus, they want to take over whatever business this gang is into."

"Great, that's all we need. A gang war."

"Exactly. Stay safe."

Layke stiffened. "Wait. Can you put more protection detail on Murray and Gabe?"

"Already on it. Scarlet is organizing a unit now, along with Martha's help."

"Good. I gotta get back to Hannah."

"Understood. Chat later."

Layke disconnected and made his way to Hannah's room.

And stopped in his tracks.

The young man from the waiting room stood holding her IV line, getting ready to add something from a syringe into the mix.

Layke took a step. "Stop! Police!"

The man pressed the syringe.

Layke leaped across the chair and tackled the man to the floor. They became entwined in a duel for power. A lamp crashed, the sound resonating throughout the room. Layke gained control and hauled the man to his feet. However, the young guy proved to be stronger than Layke anticipated and shoved him into the wall. He held Layke in a chokehold.

Struggling for breath, Layke threw his palm upward into the man's chin. Hard. The assailant released his hold and stumbled backward. It was enough to free Layke and he whipped out his gun. "Stand down!"

The doctor and nurse rushed into the room.

"Quick! He added something to Hannah's IV!" Even though only seconds had passed, Layke knew enough had probably transferred into her system to do harm.

Dr. Hobbs pulled it from her arm, not caring about the blood appearing from her exposed vein. They needed to get whatever it was out, and fast.

Layke held his gun on the man. "Lay on the floor. Hands behind your head."

The man smiled and tilted his head as if mocking Layke.

"Now!" Layke raised his gun higher. "I. Will. Shoot." Well, not really, but he needed to dominate the situation at hand.

The man hesitated but finally obeyed.

Layke reholstered his gun and put his knee on the man's back, pulling his arms behind him. He turned to the nurse. "Call 911." He pulled out his cuffs and secured the prisoner. He heaved him up and shoved him in a chair. "What did you put in her IV?"

Once again, the man smirked.

Layke pulled out his weapon. "Don't tempt me."

"Only a little cocktail I invented, but mostly ethylene glycol."

Dr. Hobbs gasped. "What? That will kill her."

"That's what they wanted."

Layke held the gun to the man's temple. "They?"

He shrugged. "Don't know. Don't care. There was a hit on the dark web—$500,000 for her death."

Layke turned to Dr. Hobbs. "Did any get in her bloodstream?"

"Her blood needs to be tested to know for sure. I'm going to start a fresh IV and give her a shot of fomepizole. That should neutralize it in a few days."

"Days?"

Dr. Hobbs grabbed the drug from a nearby cabinet and inserted it directly into Hannah's arm. He then hooked up another IV bag to Hannah's vein.

"We need to get her back to Canada, Doc."

"Understood. You must get her blood tested to ensure the poison is gone. I'll be back in a bit to check on her."

Layke stole a peek at Hannah. His pulse raced at the sight of the woman arresting his heart.

Lord, if You're listening. I know I don't talk to You much, but Hannah loves You. She's one of Yours. Please save her.

Would God hear his desperate plea?

The man beside him coughed, reminding Layke of his presence.

"Tell me, did the Martells or a man named Broderick hire you?"

"Who? I told you. I don't know. The ad on the web just posted a picture and the reward for her death."

"How did you find us?"

"Someone added your location on the dark web."

What? They were being tracked, but how?

Or…a mole slithered somewhere in their departments.

Hannah opened her groggy eyes and tried to focus. A white ceiling stared back at her. Where was she? And why did her chest feel like a ten-pound barbell held her down?

The shot!

Right. The last thing she remembered was trying to outrun machine gun fire from men on snowmobiles.

Was Layke okay? The sudden thought of him ripped from her life brought more weight to her chest. She moaned and turned her head to the right.

That's when she saw him.

Her handsome constable was sleeping sitting up in a chair.

Hers? Hardly.

"Layke?" Her groggy voice squeaked out his name.

He stirred and straightened. "You're awake." He took her hand in his. "Hey, beautiful."

Beautiful was not how she felt. "What happened?"

"Let's just say you were shot by men on snowmobiles and almost poisoned to death."

"What?"

He moved a curl off her face. "Yes, it's been an interesting few hours. Someone put a hit out on your life."

Gabe's face popped into her mind and she tried to sit up. "Gabe!"

Layke eased her back against the pillow. "Rest. Gabe

is fine. Elias's wife and Scarlet have organized a unit to protect Murray's household, including Gabe."

"Tell me more." Hannah listened as Layke told her about the attack on her life, Rob's brother and the mafia ties. "So, what business is this Martell gang in?"

"We're not entirely sure, but we do know they don't like whatever this Broderick is mining."

"Did the young man who attacked me talk?"

Layke shook his head. "Only that a ransom was put out on the dark web. The state troopers took him away an hour ago."

"Why would anyone want to kill me?"

"You protected Gabe, and they obviously didn't like that."

She pursed her lips. "We need to get back to him. I'm worried."

"We will. Tomorrow morning. Dr. Hobbs said your blood needs to be retested once we arrive at Murray's. I've arranged for a doctor to come there as I don't trust any other clinics."

A thought tumbled through her mind. "How do they keep finding us?"

He lifted his chin as his nostrils flared. "I don't know. That's been bothering me, too. I'm scared we have a leak in one of our departments."

"No way! Everyone I work with is trustworthy and like family."

"Well, I can't say the same as I don't know the officers here in the Yukon, but they seem fine." He held up her cell phone. "Doyle has been calling nonstop. Are you sure he's not more than just a boss?"

"What? Hardly. He's too old for me and is more like a father figure. Plus, he's married. Why? You jealous?"

Layke smiled and sank back into the chair. "Maybe."

What did he mean? Could he—

She stopped and ran her hand along her stomach. No. She couldn't fall for this man. She chewed the inside of her mouth.

"What is it? Tell me what's wrong."

She turned her head away from him. "I can't. Just like you can't tell me your secrets."

She heard him sigh before she drifted back to sleep.

FOURTEEN

Hannah woke to dogs barking outside and eased herself up in the comfy queen-size bed. A fire roared in the small fireplace in her bedroom at Murray and Natalie's—probably Layke's doing. Ever since they had returned to the ranch two days ago, he'd been attentive to her, ensuring she stay in bed while he worked with Elias and Doyle on the case. She insisted he keep her updated, but so far there were no new developments or intel on Broderick and the Martell mafia. Murray and Natalie's mood had turned to panic at the thought of their son. The longer he was without them, the harder it would be for him to cope.

The doctor who had visited her at the ranch took her blood to have analyzed. Thankfully, since Layke had acted quickly that day, the poison was now out of her system. She dreaded the thought of what could have happened if he hadn't have come in when he did. God's protection over her sent goose bumps racing through her body.

She pulled the homemade plaid quilt off her and eased her feet onto the hardwood floor. She expected it to be cool and was surprised by the cozy feeling. She relaxed at the warmth claiming her toes.

The pitter-patter of approaching feet startled her, and she grabbed the housecoat at the end of the bed. A knock sounded. "Come in."

Gabe bounded into the room and jumped on her bed. "Miss Hannah, it's time to get up!" He bounced up and down.

Hannah giggled.

A moment later, Layke tapped on the open door. "Safe to come in?"

"Yes," she said.

Layke entered carrying a tray of croissants, fruit and a mug of steaming hazelnut coffee.

Her favorite. She'd know that aroma anywhere. "What's this?"

"Breakfast for a special person. It's been two days and you need a more solid meal plan." His lips curved into a delightful smile.

Her heart ricocheted and a lump formed in her throat, robbing her of speech. This handsome man had stolen her attention, and she couldn't stop the feeling bubbling inside her despite her resolution to stay single forever.

God, what are You doing?

"Sport, Miss Hannah needs her rest." He turned to her. "Back into bed. Time to eat."

She saluted him and climbed back in bed and patted the spot beside her. "Gabe, join me."

He crawled under the covers and eyed Layke's tray. "Can I have some?"

Layke tilted his head. "You already had pancakes."

Gabe rubbed his tummy. "I'm still hungry."

Layke placed the tray over Hannah. She picked up a strawberry and handed it to the boy. "Here you go." She took a sip of coffee. "This is so good."

"Murray's special beans, but I made it." Layke's eyes grinned back at her.

"You did? Thanks."

"Anything for you." His whispered voice could still be heard above the roaring fire.

And it warmed her heart.

"Okay, sport. Let's leave Miss Hannah to her breakfast. How about we go feed the dogs?"

Gabe jumped out of bed. "Yes!"

Layke winked. "Rest a bit more and come down if you're able. I need to talk to you about a new development."

"I'll be there. I'm feeling much better."

"How's the shoulder?"

She rubbed it and readjusted the sling holding it in place. "Coming along."

A jealous thought raced through her. "Where's Scarlet?"

"She left yesterday. Had to get back to Whitehorse, but we're still protected by other officers."

She rejoiced inwardly with the fact she had him all to herself again.

Well, there was Gabe and all the others.

Two hours later, after getting cleaned up, Hannah made her way gingerly down the wooden staircase. A commotion led her to the dining room area where she found Layke, Doyle and Elias sitting around the table with laptops set up. Seemed like a makeshift command center. "Did you start the party without me?"

Her boss turned at her approach and jumped up. "Little one! I'm glad to see you alive and well." He pulled her into his arms. "I was so scared when I heard you were shot." He squeezed harder.

She yelped. "You're hurting me, Doyle. Still tender."

He backed away. "I'm so sorry." He brushed a curl away from her face.

Layke cleared his throat and pulled out a chair for her beside him. "Have a seat and we'll fill you in."

She smirked at his obvious overprotectiveness. "Good to have you all here. How's Martha?"

"Holding down the fort in Beaver Creek. She's a huge help to us."

The woman had come from a wealthy family but severed ties when she and Elias fell in love years ago. Her family didn't approve, and she didn't care. Hannah longed for a love like that someday.

But now it would never happen. She set the thoughts aside and concentrated on the team. "What have I missed out on?"

Layke turned his computer screen toward her. "First, Gabe finally confessed to knowing what the boys have been mining. Diamonds."

"What?" She frowned. "How did you get that out of him?"

"Don't worry. I didn't coerce him. We just had a friendly chat, and he said he was scared to tell us earlier because he overheard the gang talking about it and they caught him. They warned him that if he said anything, they would hurt his friends."

"Where is he now?"

"Outside with Murray and Natalie building a fort. Officers are standing guard."

Her heart ached to be with him. She shoved the thought aside and concentrated on the screen. "So what do we know about these diamonds?"

"Only that diamond mining happens in the Northwest Territories, right, Elias?"

The older gentlemen took a sip from his mug before answering. "Yes, there's mostly gold mining in the Yukon. I had heard of a rare diamond deposit, but no mining here. I'm shocked this gang discovered some in this cave."

"And we still don't know where that is, right?" Hannah asked.

Doyle shuffled some papers. "No, but I did hear again from my informant about another smuggling happening tonight back in Beaver Creek."

Layke narrowed his eyes. "And you trust him after we were ambushed at the last one?"

He shrugged. "Don't have a choice, do we? We're out of leads."

He had them there.

She stood. "When do we leave?"

Layke bolted out of his chair. "Whoa now. You're not going anywhere in your condition."

She crossed her arms. "You're not stopping me from seeing this through. I'm fine. My strength is back."

"How can you possibly raise your weapon and shoot?"

"You need me to be there if we find more boys."

Doyle stood. "We can handle it, little one."

"Hardly. You need my help with the kids." She turned to Layke. "I can shoot fine. My right arm wasn't hurt. Plus, I excelled at the firing range, remember, boss man?"

"She's right. I've seen her shoot," Doyle said.

Elias gathered his computer. "We need to finish our plan and then roll, so we can make it in time. We have a bit of a drive."

Layke sighed and pointed in her direction. "Fine, but you'll stay out of the line of fire. I'll go tell Murray and the officers we'll be leaving soon."

Five hours later after formulating a plan and driving to Beaver Creek, they hunkered down at the CBSA station. They'd secured the crossing with constables and border patrol agents hidden at various points on the highway. Each officer was heavily armed with a variety of weaponry. Doyle appointed her to man the booth as cars approached.

Layke shook his head and crossed his arms. "He's putting you right in the middle of it."

"I'll be fine. It's my job, Layke. I know what I'm doing, or do you not trust in my abilities?"

"It's not you I don't trust." He eyed Doyle.

"Why don't you like him?"

"He's too personal with you and rubs me the wrong way."

"I told you. He took me under his wing when I first moved to the Yukon. Taught me this job. I don't know what I'd do without him." She put on her parka. "It's time to go. The truck should be crossing at any time now. Remember, Layke. God's got this."

His handsome face contorted. "Where was He when you got shot?"

"Right there with me. I could have died."

Layke opened his mouth to say something and, instead, closed it. He checked the chamber in his Smith & Wesson before slamming it shut and holstering it. He strapped a machine gun over his shoulder. "Let's go. You stay in the booth."

Hannah walked out into the cold and around the corner into the booth, which was detached from the station. She knew he meant well and was only being overprotective because she'd been hurt, but she could do this. She *had* to do this. For all those innocent children.

Layke crouched beside a cruiser with Elias and other constables.

Hannah uttered a desperate prayer. "Father, keep us safe. Help us to end this today. Protect those boys."

A roaring engine filled the night, but no truck headlights approached. What was that noise?

Ignoring Layke's order, she stepped outside.

The hum deepened.

Layke and Elias stood.

A light appeared in the sky and brightened as it approached.

"Drone! Get down, Hannah!" Layke yelled.

The drone peppered the area with multiple shots.

Lights bobbled from the distant tree line, indicating

that gang members were advancing toward their location at high speed.

The drone reapproached.

She dove back into the booth and winced when she fell onto her wounded shoulder.

The unmanned aerial vehicle fired a missile into the station, exploding the building.

"Hannah!" Layke fired at the approaching men and raced toward her booth, which was yards away from the now demolished border station. He had to get to her. It was the second time she'd put herself in harm's way and he didn't like it. The need to protect her washed over him again, catching him off guard. This woman had stolen his heart in a matter of days.

Along with Gabe. The eight-year-old with the big brown eyes.

The hum returned, announcing the beast's presence, along with an additional round of shots. It fired another missile at the highway. The pavement exploded into pieces and left behind a massive hole in the road.

Layke raised the MP5 submachine gun and aimed it toward the drone. He waited for the perfect time and pulled the trigger, firing multiple shots.

The drone exploded, lighting the darkened sky. Its pieces shattered to the ground.

Shouts from the field alerted him to the gang's lethal intentions. They had to get out of there. They were outnumbered and with nowhere to hide. Who had sold them out? The informant?

Layke stepped into the booth. Glass crunched beneath his boots.

Hannah was huddled in the corner, holding her hands over her head. She looked up at him and cried out.

He pulled her into his arms. "You're okay." He released her. "We need to move. Now."

"Doyle?"

"He's fine. So is Elias, but armed men are approaching from the woods and we don't have cover. The building is gone. The road is obliterated. No one is getting across the border now."

Her eyes widened. "What about the other officers?"

"They can't get to us because the highway is destroyed. We're on our own."

Elias approached with Doyle. "Someone planned this out perfectly."

"But who?" Doyle asked.

"We don't have time to figure that out right now." Layke pointed to the men running through the field. "They're almost here."

Elias pulled out his keys. "Let's take the back roads into the detachment in Beaver Creek. We can beat them there."

A shot rang out and they dove for cover. Who had fired? Most of the men haven't reached them yet. Layke lifted his head and spotted a lone figure skulking behind a tree a few yards away. "Look at your five o'clock. Must have been a scout, checking the area. I have a plan." Layke quickly shared his intentions.

Doyle grabbed Hannah's hand. "Let's go."

Layke and Elias raised their guns, firing into the night.

Doyle and Hannah raced to the cruiser and climbed inside.

Elias fired as Layke crouched low and circled around the flattened building toward the nearby trees, positioning himself behind the shooter. As discussed, Elias stopped shooting. Hopefully, he too had reached the cruiser. Layke raised his weapon and snuck behind the man.

A branch snapped beneath his boot. He stopped.

The man turned.

Layke plowed into him, knocking the suspect to the ground.

He shoved his gun into the man's chest. "Stand down."

The cruiser pulled up beside them and Elias opened the passenger door. "Get in!"

Layke hauled the suspect up and grabbed the rifle from his hand before pushing him into the back seat beside Doyle.

Doyle pointed his gun at the man. "Don't try anything." He pulled off the assailant's mask.

Elias sped along the back roads with Hannah directing him to the detachment.

They rushed into the building as Constable Antoine pulled in behind them.

Where had he come from? Suspicion crept into Layke's bones as hairs danced at the back of his neck. He only trusted Hannah. No one else.

The constable approached. "Hey, what's going on?"

"Didn't you hear the explosions at the border?"

"No. I just came on shift. What happened?" He pointed to the man they had in custody. "Who's that?"

"Hopefully, information in stopping this gang."

"Okay, I'll get the interrogation room ready for you. Bring him this way." He walked away, followed by Doyle and Elias. Martha waved to them from the reception area.

Hannah rubbed her bottom lip. "What are you thinking?"

"That was too convenient. He's just coming on shift now? Odd timing."

"Maybe he had an appointment or something."

Layke harrumphed and crossed his arms. "Possibly." He gestured toward the room. "Shall we find out what we can from this guy?"

"I'll be there in a minute. I want to check on Gabe." She grabbed her cell phone and moved down the hall.

Layke walked into the interrogation room.

Doyle had the suspect shoved against the wall.

"Whoa. What's going on?" Layke pulled Doyle off the man. "We need information from him. What are you doing?"

"He tried to kill my girl."

"Your girl? You mean your *employee*." Why did this superintendent irk Layke so much?

"I've known her much longer than you, Constable."

Elias raised his hands. "Guys, this isn't getting us anywhere." He shoved the man back into the chair and cuffed his hands to the metal bar. "There. Stay put."

Layke reeled in his anger and pulled up a chair. "Tell us your name."

"I'd rather not." He jiggled the cuffs. "Let me go, or they will come after me and kill all of you."

Elias sat. "Who are they?"

Hannah walked in and leaned against the wall.

The man eyed her. "I'll only talk to her and you, Constable Jackson."

"Why?"

"Don't trust anyone but you."

"And why do you trust us?" Hannah asked.

"I have my reasons." He jiggled the cuffs again. "What do you say?"

Layke huffed and sat back. "Guys, can you give us the room?"

Doyle and Elias left.

Layke shoved a chair toward Hannah. "You need to sit. You're white."

"You feeling better from your hospital visit, Officer Morgan?" The man smirked.

Layke's face heated as anger threatened to bubble to the surface. He counted in his head slowly to ward it off.

After reaching ten, he pulled out a notebook. "Tell us your name."

"Smitty."

"Smitty? That's it?" Hannah asked.

"Yup. What else do you want to know?"

"Tell us about Broderick." Layke positioned his pen.

"Don't know much. He's the head of the ring. Takes kids from various events to help him mine for diamonds."

"How does he pick the boys?"

"He usually grabs them when they're on retreats. You know. Scouts, church outings, campfires, etc."

Layke rubbed the knot forming in his shoulder muscles at the news of how the operation grabbed the children. He needed to save these boys and stop the child labor. And fast. "So he doesn't just pick orphans?"

"No. Any boys that meet his height criteria."

Layke glanced at Hannah. Her normally pleasant face had shifted into one of pain and anger. It was clear she had a heart for children. He focused back on Smitty. "So, the right height to fit into the cave?"

"Correct."

"To mine for diamonds."

"Correct."

Could he not provide more than one-word answers? Layke gritted his teeth. "Tell us what's going on with the Martell mafia. Are they connected to your ring?"

Smitty's eyes widened and he bit his lip.

Something scared him.

"What is it?" Hannah leaned forward. "You can trust us."

"They're bad news. Word on the street is they're out for blood for Broderick getting into the diamond mining business."

"Why?" Layke asked.

"The head of the Martells doesn't like anyone taking

over his precious mining monopoly. He's worked hard to build his empire."

"You mean Perry Martell. The politician? His business is diamond smuggling?"

Smitty nodded. "But you didn't hear that from me. He'd put a hit on me if he knew I told you. He tries to portray a good image, but everyone knows he's bad news."

"Can you provide us with the location of Broderick's diamond mine?" Layke asked.

Smitty raised a brow. "What will you give me in exchange?"

Layke glanced at Hannah. He hated to give a criminal a promise, but they needed to find these kids. "We'll see what we can do. Perhaps the judge will lighten your sentence if he knew you cooperated and helped us bring down both gangs."

"As long as you keep my name out of the news."

"We will."

"Get me a map of the area and I'll show you."

Hannah stood. "I'll go brief Doyle and Elias and get a map." She left the room.

"Can you tell me the location of the ranch where Broderick is keeping the kids?" Layke fingered his pen.

"Never been there, but I did hear some of the others talking about it. I can give you a radius but not an actual location."

That's more than they had before. Layke would take it.

Moments later, Hannah returned with a map. She spread it out on the table. "Okay, show us." She handed him a marker.

Smitty jiggled the cuffs. "Can't with these on."

Layke stood and pulled out his keys. "Don't try anything."

"You think I'd want to be on the street now that I told

you all this? Not a chance. I'll take prison over being on Broderick or the Martell's radar."

Layke removed the cuffs but kept his hand on his weapon.

Smitty circled a spot on the map. "Here's the diamond mine. The road only goes a kilometer into the location. You will need to walk through rough terrain to get to the cave. It's due north." He then circled a bigger radius. "The ranch is somewhere here. It's pretty remote."

"Anything else you can tell us?" Hannah asked.

Smitty's eyes darkened. "Yes. Watch your back and don't trust anyone. Not even those on the force."

Layke flinched.

Hannah fell back into her chair.

They both got the message.

Trust no one.

FIFTEEN

Layke tightened his Kevlar vest and checked the MP5 submachine gun while other task force members locked and loaded supplies in preparation of their takedown at the diamond mine. It wasn't far from their current location, so at least they had that in their favor. He stuffed several pieces of equipment, ammunition and a personal locator beacon in the duffel bag. *Always be prepared.* The motto his sergeant had instilled in his brain. Elias and Doyle left to scope out the area, taking other officers with them. Constables Antoine and Yellowhead would drive in the lead cruiser, followed by Hannah and Layke.

He glanced at Hannah. Her ashen face told him pain still plagued her body. Could she really withstand the stress of this takedown?

Layke touched her arm. "You should sit this one out. Let us handle it." He added a gun to an ankle holster. This case had proved to him that he needed the added protection. Just in case.

"No! I need to be there if the kids are in the mine."

"It's six o'clock. Do you really think they'll be there at this hour in the dark?"

She shrugged. "I can't take the chance. I'm fine. Just a bit of pain."

"You look like you're ready to drop."

She took a sip of her coffee and held up the cup. "Nothing a little caffeine won't rectify."

He pursed his lips. "I don't like it, Hannah."

"You don't have a choice. I will not let these kids down."

"You'll make a great mother one day."

She stared at the floor before glancing back at him with dull eyes. Something had saddened her, but what? Didn't she want to be a mother?

"What is it, Hannah?"

She cleared her throat and pulled out her weapon. "It's nothing." She checked her chamber and slammed it shut. "We need to get the troops rolling. Kids' lives are depending on us."

"Fine." He grabbed his coat as his cell phone rang. Unknown caller. "Constable Jackson here."

"Constable, this is Donald Crawford calling back."

Layke snapped his fingers to get Hannah's attention. "Mr. Crawford, I'm going to put you on speakerphone." He pressed the button and held the phone between them. "Officer Morgan is here with me. What can we do for you?"

The man cleared his throat. "I know you probably did a search on me, so I wanted to call you back. I did not kidnap that child. I promise. I lost my temper with a news reporter and hit her in the leg with a stick. She charged me, but I got off with community service."

"Okay, so can you tell me if you received a ransom call?" Layke said.

"No. Nothing."

Hannah shifted her stance. "So why not tell us the first time we spoke to you?"

"I'm sorry. I couldn't talk freely. I was in a meeting room and had you on speakerphone when my staff came in."

Nothing in his tone revealed deceit, but could they trust this man's word?

Layke wondered if they'd ever get a break. Hopefully, the cave search would be valuable to the case. "Thanks for calling us back. Let us know if you do hear from anyone."

"I will. Please find my boy."

"We're doing our best." Layke clicked off the call. "Well, that answers our questions about him."

"Yup. Did you hear anything back from Trooper Allard?"

"Just that there were no further developments. Cash's apartment was wiped clean."

"Figures. More dead ends. We gotta roll." She put on a Kevlar vest but struggled with the straps.

"Let me help you with that." He fastened it around her waist, gazing into her eyes at the same time. "Hannah, about earlier. You can trust me." He caressed her cheek and pulled her closer to him.

She let out a soft sigh. "I know. It's not you." She backed away, picked up her parka and scurried out of the room.

What was he doing? He would not start something.

His head told him that, but his heart had already fallen. Hard.

He sighed and walked out the door.

Thirty minutes later, Hannah and Layke pulled in behind other law enforcement vehicles. The area was flooded with activity. They would need to walk the rest of the way. Half a kilometer in rough terrain…according to Smitty. Each officer was equipped with the necessary tools to search the darkened area.

"You ready?" Layke asked.

"Yes." She stepped from the vehicle.

The group made their way through the densely wooded area and hilly ground. Local officers led the pack, with Hannah and Layke holding up the rear. Thankfully, they all wore night goggles or they wouldn't be able to see anything.

Ahead of him, Hannah stumbled and teetered. He rushed forward and caught her before she fell. "Got you."

"Thanks." She regained her footing and kept walking.

God, keep us safe. Give Hannah strength.

Wait—what? He was praying now? Hannah must be a good influence on him. Could he trust God with his life?

He flinched. He wasn't ready to surrender. Would he ever? He needed to control every situation in his life and couldn't trust his circumstances with someone he couldn't see.

An officer ahead of them whistled.

Their clue to say they were there and to be ready for anything.

Layke tensed and lifted his weapon, preparing for an assault.

The group positioned themselves behind trees around the entrance to the small cave. They almost didn't see it, but Smitty had told them what to look for. An opening in the side of the mountain covered with cut brush. The gang's way of hiding it every night.

Hannah stood behind a snow-laden Douglas fir with her weapon raised. A wind rose, picking up her curls and thrusting them into array. She pulled her tuque down farther on her head.

He ignored the feelings rising and took a position beside her. He wouldn't stray far from her side, his protective senses on high alert. No way would he make the same mistake he'd made with Amber. She had tried to discredit his policing abilities and make him look bad, so he'd pulled back on a mission and left her side for a brief moment, ignoring his rule to never leave a fellow officer. It had been enough time for the perpetrator to act, and she'd paid the price for his stupidity. She hadn't deserved death even though she had betrayed him. Images of her open, lifeless eyes flooded his mind, but he pushed it aside. He had to concentrate on this mission.

They waited for movement.

None came.

Constable Antoine signaled for them to advance.

Someone lit the portable flood light.

"Police! Come out with your hands up," Constable Antoine yelled.

They were greeted with the howl of a coyote. Then another. Otherwise, the area remained silent.

"Move in!" Constable Antoine rushed forward and moved the branches away from the mouth of the cave.

Hannah and Layke stepped out from their hiding place. Once they knew the area was clear, they holstered their weapons.

"Okay, who wants to crawl into the cave?" Layke asked.

No one volunteered.

Really?

"Fine, I will." Layke moved forward, knelt in front of the opening and pulled out his Maglite.

Hannah crouched beside him. "You're not going alone. We're partners, remember?"

He nodded and crawled in.

He shone his light and whistled. "No wonder they needed children." His face flushed as the thought brought a rush of anger. The low ceiling sparkled with the promise of rewards beyond anyone's imagination.

Short-handled pics and shovels lay in different spots around them. Tunnels snaked off in various directions. He pointed. "Those probably lead to more mining caves." He moved closer in an attempt to get a better look.

"I can't believe they made children do their dirty work. All for a quick buck."

"I know. Maddening." Innocent children stolen from their loved ones for one man's greed. Why?

"What now?" Hannah flattened herself as she made her way around the juts in the ceiling.

"We need to get forensics in here and—"

A flashing light illuminating one of the tunnels caught his attention. "Shh."

Tick. Tick. Tick.

That sound could only mean one thing. Their arrival had been anticipated. "Get out! Now!"

They shimmied their way back through the entrance and bolted upright.

"Bomb! Everyone get back!" Layke grabbed Hannah's hand and propelled her forward.

The explosion rocked the mountainside.

Debris rained in every direction.

Layke tackled Hannah, throwing himself on top of her. She yelped.

He knew he'd hurt her shoulder, but he needed to shield the woman of the dreams he never thought he wanted.

A rumble sounded in the distance.

Not good.

He shone his light toward the sound and gasped.

"Avalanche!"

Hannah ignored the pain exploding through her shoulder and raced through the woods, branches smacking her face. She ignored the sting and kept running. They only had a matter of minutes to get out of the avalanche's deadly path. How would they make it back to their vehicles without being smothered with tons of snow? *Lord, give us haste and make us light-footed. Protect us.* Would God answer her rushed prayer after her doubts the past few days? *Trust.* There was that word again. She hadn't stopped loving God, despite struggling with not only His sovereignty but her identity in Him.

A verse from Psalms popped into her head, reminding

her that God had made her in her mother's womb, marvelous in His image. He knew every bone in her body. It didn't matter she couldn't conceive or that she had never known the woman who gave birth to her. She was a beautiful creation in His sight. *Thank You, Lord, for this reminder. Forgive me for doubting.* Resolved in her identity, she ran faster. She needed to get back to Gabe. Back to who she really was. A child of the One True King.

Bouncing lights appeared ahead of her as officers raced through the brush. They'd gotten a head start since they were farther away from the explosion. She could hear Layke's heavy breathing behind her but couldn't stop to see his location. His pounding footsteps revealed his close proximity.

The rumble behind them grew louder, which meant they were running out of time.

Precious time.

Lord, please!

In record minutes, the group reached the clearing and hopped into their vehicles, speeding back onto the side road.

Layke raced in front of her and opened the Jeep doors. "Get in! Quick!"

She scrambled into the front seat and Layke started the engine.

Hannah peeked out but only darkness greeted her.

Layke backed up, and as he turned onto the roadway Hannah caught a glimpse of the pending white cover of doom in the Jeep's headlights.

She hit the console. "Go! Go! Go!"

The tires spun on the icy road.

They would never make it.

God! Help us!

The tires continued to spin, not gaining any traction. Their hope of escape diminished.

Her pulse hammered in her head and she was sure Layke would hear it.

"Please, God!" she yelled.

The tires broke free and the Jeep lunged forward but not fast enough.

A heavy blanket of snow battered their vehicle, smothering them.

They were too late.

They were buried alive.

SIXTEEN

Layke struggled to breathe, his head pounding from lack of oxygen. Dread crept in like a poisonous scorpion ready to pounce on its prey. Uncontrollable shivers attacked his body as he gripped the door handle. He needed to escape this tomb. He took a breath. In. Out. His pulse quickened. Had his fear of being buried alive just come true? It couldn't be.

A whimper sounded beside him.

Hannah.

Get a grip, Layke. You've got this.

His head continued to throb.

Who was he kidding? His childhood fear came rushing back, and he pictured himself at the bottom of a freshly dug grave he'd fallen into while running away from his mother. They had come to tend to his grandmother's headstone when he'd refused to help his mother replace the dead flowers. The cemetery scared him, and she had dragged him there against his wishes. He ran away from her, but didn't see the unmarked grave and fell into it. Soil had toppled in on him when the groundskeeper found him. After that episode, nightmares of being buried alive plagued his sleep.

And now it was coming true.

He closed his eyes and rested his head. It wasn't like he could see anything in the darkened vehicle anyway.

A hand touched his shoulder. "You okay?"

"Can't breathe."

He heard her inhale a mechanical breath. Then another. Right. She was asthmatic.

And here he was stressing about not breathing. *Get a grip.*

He fumbled for his Maglite and turned it on, shining it at Hannah. "You okay?"

She nodded, but her wild eyes told him she too struggled to remain in control.

It was up to him to save them. He pulled out his cell phone.

No signal.

Of course, there wouldn't be under the mountain of snow.

Think, Layke, think.

How long could they survive buried under this much snow? He took another deep breath and exhaled slowly. He could do this.

He remembered a tool he had stuck in the duffel bag before leaving the detachment. He popped forward. "That's it!"

"What?"

"I need to get into the back."

"Why?"

"Personal locator device I found at the detachment with all the other equipment. I packed it before we came. Just in case." Now he had to get to it to turn it on.

"Is it in the back?"

"Yes."

She unbuckled her seat belt. "I'm smaller. I'll do it."

He winced. "Your shoulder though."

"Compared to being buried alive? I think it will be fine." She climbed over the console and into the back seat. She pulled the seat down.

"It's on the right side in the duffel bag."

She shimmied through the opening.

He held his breath and waited.

Would she be able to find it?

If so, would the signal beacon be found under mounds of snow?

God, if You're there, help us survive this. I promise if You do, I'll give my life to You.

Could he really bargain with God?

"Got it!" Hannah crawled back through the hole and into the front seat. She handed it to him.

Thank You, God.

Now all He had to do was bring someone to rescue them.

"Okay, let's turn this on."

Hannah grabbed his hand. "Let's pray."

"Go ahead."

She tilted her head. "What? No objections."

"Not from me."

She smiled and closed her eyes. "Lord, You've brought us this far and I refuse to believe You won't protect us now. Bring someone to find us and help us locate the children. In Jesus' name, Amen."

"Amen."

She released her hold on his hand.

He turned on the device. The light blinked a steady rhythm.

Matching his heartbeat.

Questions jumbled through his mind. Would he get out of here alive? Would he find Noel and see Murray again? Just when he'd found them.

Hannah rubbed his arm. "What are you thinking?"

He rested his head back and turned toward her. Was this his moment of confession? He had to tell someone his secret. "Just that I wouldn't get to know the half brother I've just discovered."

"Will you tell me your story?"

"I've never told anyone my secrets. Not even my best friend, Hudson."

She squeezed his bicep. "I won't tell anyone. I promise."

Right then, in his mind, he threw his rule book away. He didn't need it. He wouldn't live his life etched in rules any longer. He'd follow his heart.

He placed the glowing flashlight on the dash.

"My mom started beating me when I was six years old."

She snapped her hand back. "What? What kind of mother would do that?"

"I know. The first time was simply because I wanted to go to the park with the other boys and when she didn't let me, I pouted. Something in her snapped. Then the beatings increased with every supposed bad thing I did. Didn't pick up my toys, got a B minus, forgot to take out the trash. I couldn't do anything right, so I stopped trying. I finally ran away when I was fourteen and lived on the street for a bit. That's when I met Hudson."

"What happened?"

"The police found me when I turned fifteen and took me back to live with my mom. She was filled with rage at the embarrassment I caused her, so she tried to hit me, but I stopped her. Hit her back."

"What?"

"I know. I know. It was wrong and I never did it again. It made her stop though. She started going to church and became a Christian. However, I couldn't bring myself to forgive her. Hudson tried to get me to go to his church, but I refused."

"Then you went into law enforcement."

"Yes. Shortly after I did a search for my father."

"So that's when you found him?"

"No. I couldn't locate him. I gave up and concentrated on becoming a good cop. It was only after I moved to Calgary that I found him through one of those ancestry kits and—"

Could he go on? Would she think the sins of his father were on him?

"What is it, Layke? You can tell me. I heard you say he was in prison for murder."

"Not just one. Multiple murders."

She gasped.

He turned away from her.

"Not what I expected you to say." She paused. "Layke, that's not on you. You're a good man."

He turned back to her. The flashlight's beam sparkled in her eyes.

"Thank you."

"Did you go visit him?"

"I tried this past summer, but he wouldn't see me. Even after Murray tried to convince him, he refused. Murray and I have been in constant touch since."

"And when he called you about Noel being kidnapped, you rushed here. That's so noble of you. Wanting to help your new family in their time of trouble."

"I had to."

"Did you ever forgive your mother?"

"She's tried to contact me through social media, but I've ignored her."

"Maybe God is telling you something different now, huh?"

"Maybe."

Was He? Had He put Hannah in his life to soften him. And Gabe? Should he tell her all of his secrets?

"There's more." He took off his gloves and rubbed his chilly hands together. Was he stalling? *Tell her. Before it's too late.* "I promised myself never to get involved with anyone because of my mother, but it's not only as a result of her beatings and deceit. My second year on the force I got a new partner. Amber Maurier. I was smitten by her good looks. Everyone was, but it appeared that she liked me. I was shocked and humbled."

"Wait. Why would you be shocked? You're an amazing and handsome man."

He raked his hand through his wavy hair. "I didn't see that. Still don't, really. Anyway, she played me to get ahead in her career. Made it look like I doctored evidence, which I did not. She did it to get me fired, so she could take my place at our detachment and move up. During a stakeout a year ago, I left her side as I was so angry to be in her presence. Something went wrong and she ended up getting shot. It was all my fault. I haven't been able to forgive myself for that mistake. I vowed I would never trust another woman again after what she and my mother did to me."

He shifted in his seat and turned his body toward the redhead. "And then you came into my life and rocked my world. I—"

A curl escaped from behind her tuque.

He entwined it between his fingers, letting his hand linger close to her cheek.

How could he have doubted his feelings for this amazing woman?

His heart hitched, stealing words from his mouth but opening wide.

Yes, he could finally move on from his past wounds and give his all.

Would Hannah let him in? He hoped so as suddenly thoughts of marriage and children with her filled his mind.

He moved closer and stared at her lush lips.

Her eyes widened and she pulled back. "I can't."

His bruised heart sank.

* * *

Hannah clamped her eyes shut. There was nothing she wanted more than to feel the handsome officer's lips on hers, but she would not start something she couldn't finish. He deserved someone who could bear children.

And she couldn't.

A tear rolled down her cheek.

Layke brushed it away. "Hannah, will you tell me why you're so sad?"

Could she? After all, he'd let her in on his secrets.

"Tell me. Did you have a bad relationship with someone?"

Well, there was that. Colt had scarred her from trusting men, but that wasn't what was now holding her back from giving Layke her heart.

"I did. In college."

"What was his name?"

"Colt. He swept me off my feet like all fairy tales start, but I soon discovered his deep, dark secret. I almost lost my life because of it."

"What?"

The image of that frightful night flashed in her mind. The darkness in Colt's eyes haunted her dreams still to this day. After discovering his secret, she'd tried to get away from his lair. However, he had other plans. It was too late for her to escape. He had taken her away from the college under the cover of darkness with evil intentions. However, God had other plans.

"My first real boyfriend almost raped me."

"What?"

"Yes. There was a rapist running rampant in our college, but I had no idea it was Colt. Until I found his trinkets. Trinkets the news said the perpetrator took from each woman. None of the women could identify him. Until now."

Layke whistled. "What happened?"

"He caught me when I found them, and in a struggle I let one drop in my room. Kaylin found it and recognized it from a fellow student he'd attacked. She called the police."

"So, this was when you were training in the CBSA?"

"Yes. He was a spoiled rich kid who thought he wanted to become a border security officer. He moved up fast in the class and it went to his head."

"How did the police find you?"

"They didn't. I never told you, but I excelled in my defensive tactics class. I was able to overpower him and escape. I led the police to him. They arrested and convicted him under my testimony. Plus, he was in possession of the other girls' trinkets. That sealed the deal."

Layke pulled her into his arms. "I'm so sorry you went through that."

Her heart leaped at his embrace. She wished she could stay there forever.

He pulled back. "Sweet Hannah. I'm not Colt. I want you to know I would never hurt you."

She smiled and ran her finger down his face, lingering on his five-o'clock shadow. "I know."

"Then what is it?"

She sighed and pulled her hand down. How would he take the news? She couldn't hide it any longer. "I can't have children, Layke. You deserve someone better because you would make an awesome father. I can't give you that."

He jolted backward and turned his head.

But not before she noticed the look of disappointment on his face.

There, she'd done it. She'd crushed his heart.

And her own.

Layke moved back to his side of the seat. Why would she think that confession would change his feelings for her? Did she really think that little of him? Disappointment raced through him. Not because of her condition but because she thought he wouldn't love her anyway. He would make it work. Adoption was always an option.

Maybe she didn't care for him like he did her.

"Layke, I'm sorry I—"

Scratching sounded near them.

He held up his hand. "Shh." His tone was too harsh. "What's that noise?"

It grew louder.

Someone was digging.

He pounded on the door. "Help! We're in here."

Hannah joined him and banged her door. "Help us!"

"Hannah? Layke?" Corporal Bakker.

"Elias! We're here." Relief flooded through his bones, and his shoulders relaxed. God had heard his plea.

"We'll get you out. Hang on!"

Hannah grabbed his hand. "God answered my prayer."

"He did." Layke pulled his hand away.

She turned her head but not before he saw the tears.

An hour later, the officers had been able to dig them out. They had detected the signal shortly after they'd gotten out of the avalanche's path and returned with a snowplow and lots of workers to free them.

He now sat at the detachment going over topical maps. He had to find the ranch before more harm came to the children.

Hannah opened the door and peeked her head in. "Can I come in?"

He sat back. "Of course. You okay?"

"I just took some meds for the pain in my shoulder. It's throbbing."

Silence stifled the air between them.

"Listen, I wanted to thank you for your quick thinking back in the Jeep," she said.

"What do you mean?"

"You kept a clear head and remembered the locator device. My mind was mush and racing with thoughts of terror. Some Christian I am."

He had faced his fear of being buried alive. Plus, he had said a prayer, and now he had a bargain to live up to.

"Don't be hard on yourself. God understands."

"Look at you, talking about God."

"Right?"

"Doyle is taking me back to the ranch. I need sleep."

"Of course." He stood. "Listen, I—"

Doyle burst into the room. "You ready, Hannah?"

"Talk to you later?" she said.

"You got it. Sleep well. I'll be back soon. Just trying to figure out some things here first."

"Don't work too late. You need rest, too." She followed Doyle from the room.

He wanted to tell her how he felt but knew the timing wasn't quite right.

For the next two hours, he studied the region's maps trying to figure out how they could locate a ranch and multiple cabins. How did this gang hide so easily?

The Martells still hadn't made a move toward taking down Broderick. As far as local authorities knew, of course. And the avalanche had covered any chance of them finding evidence among the rubble the gang had inflicted.

"God—"

His cell phone rang. He grabbed it and noticed the time. One thirty in the morning. He glanced at the caller—Hannah.

He bolted out of his chair as goose bumps skirted across his arm. "What's wrong?"

"They're here," she whispered.

"Who?"

"The gang. We're under attack. Come—"

The call dropped.

Fear sliced through him and his legs weakened. He grabbed the table to steady himself as dread overtook his weary body.

He had to save Hannah and Gabe.

Before the gang stole them from him forever.

SEVENTEEN

Layke pulled onto his half brother's road, heart pounding. Hannah's Jeep fishtailed at his sharp turn. He struggled to keep the vehicle on the road with a new storm pummeling the area. *Lord, keep them safe.* Finally, after what seemed like an eternity, he approached the ranch in stealth mode by turning off the lights.

Silence greeted him. Stillness. Where was everyone? Was he too late?

He stepped out of the vehicle and removed his gun. He had to stay on high alert. Lives depended on him. He approached the police officer detached to guard the place. Layke peeked in the window of the cruiser. The constable was slumped forward. Layke opened the door and checked for a pulse.

Weak.

The gang had subdued him first. He was out cold.

"Hannah!" Layke took the front steps two at a time in spite of the falling snow. He checked the door. Unlocked. He eased it open, slipped inside and listened.

Once again, silence greeted him.

No laughter. No conversation. No barking dogs. Where were the huskies?

He raced to the living room with his weapon raised. "Police!"

Murray and Natalie lay still on their stomachs gagged with their hands tied behind their backs.

"No!" *Lord, I just found my family. Don't take them from me.* Layke rushed over and fell to the floor. He felt Murray's wrist for a pulse. Steady. Natalie. Steady.

Thank You.

He gently shook them. "Wake up!"

They both stirred.

Murray squirmed and moaned behind the duct tape on his mouth.

Layke untied and removed their gags, helping them to sit. "What happened?"

"They took Hannah and Gabe!" Murray's eyes darted back and forth.

"Slow down. Tell me what happened. Where are your dogs?"

"Tranquilized. It was feeding time and I called them, but there was no answer. That's when I knew something was wrong. They always come running. I found the officer outside unconscious and discovered the dogs inside the barn, all alive but sleeping."

Thank heavens. His brother would be crushed if something fatal happened to his dogs. They were family, as well as his livelihood.

"What about the officer inside?"

Natalie sobbed. "They tranquilized him, too, and stuffed him in a closet."

"Hannah tried to stop them, but they knocked her unconscious." Murray rubbed a welt on his forehead. "That's when some of them took her and Gabe away. The rest gagged us. I tried to stop them, but they hit me on the head. Next thing I knew, you were at my side."

"How many were there?"

"Five or six," Natalie said.

"How long ago did they leave?"

Murray glanced at his watch. "About ninety minutes."

Layke stood. "Do you know where they took them?"

"No. They just said everyone would pay for interfering. That's what *he* wanted." He held his hands over his face and sobbed. "I failed you, brother. Now Noel, Hannah and Gabe are lost to us."

Layke eased Murray's hands down. "You didn't, man. There was nothing you could do. Pray and pray hard."

He nodded and grabbed his wife's hands, bowing their heads.

Layke pulled out his cell phone and punched in Elias's number. He didn't care that he was getting him out of bed. He hurried outside and grabbed his laptop from the Jeep along with additional weaponry. The wind created a vortex of snow circling in front of the ranch house.

"What's going on, Layke?" Elias's groggy voice reminded Layke of the hour.

Could he trust this corporal or was he the leak? Someone knew their every step. *Lord, guide me.*

"They took Hannah and Gabe. Constable Antoine is unconscious. We need everyone here at the ranch. Stat. I have an idea on how to find them."

"What?"

Layke could hear him rustling. "Do you have connections in the military?"

"I do. Why?"

"I have a radius of where the ranch is, but need their infrared imagery to find its location."

"Do you know how big an ask that is?" Elias replied.

"I don't care. We need to find them all. Bring Hannah and those boys home. Safe."

"Okay, one of them owes me. I'll call in a favor, but it's a long shot."

Layke turned his face to the sky and closed his eyes, allowing the snowflakes to settle on his cheeks almost like it cleansed him from the guilt of letting this kidnapping happen. "Do it. How soon can you get here?"

"I'm in the area so not long. I'll call in the troops."

"Bring a medic."

"Got it. See you soon." He clicked off.

Layke stepped back inside and set his laptop on the table.

Murray sat beside him. "What's your plan?"

He pulled up an image he'd found of the region Smitty had circled on the map. He pointed, circling his finger around an area. "Our prisoner told us the ranch is somewhere in this radius. This was as small as he could narrow it down."

"I know that area. It's huge and mostly wooded." He slammed his hand on the table. "You'll never find them. It's too dense. Why did I let Noel go on that trip? What kind of a father am I?"

Layke grabbed his arm. "A good, loving one. Stop blaming yourself. This is the work of criminals."

"I'm sorry."

"Don't be." Layke gestured toward the map. "Have you been there?"

"Only by snowmobile and sled."

Layke pointed to a line on the map. "Is this a road?"

"It is, but it's probably impassable in this storm."

"Let's pray it's not."

Murray stood. "I'm coming with you."

"No, you're not. I need you to stay here with Natalie."

Natalie entered the room with a groggy Constable Yellowhead beside her. The officer had been deployed from Beaver Creek to protect them.

"Are you okay, Constable?" Layke asked.

"Angry I let them get the drop on me."

"No one saw this attack coming. How did they even

know we were here?" Layke scratched his head. There had to be a mole providing them information. Or—

"Wait! I need to check something."

Layke grabbed his flashlight and raced outside. He shone it around the entire vehicle and under it. That's when he saw it.

A tracker. Lodged deep into one of the wheel bearings. A perfect place to hide.

Layke yanked it off and squeezed it in his hand. How had the police constables missed this earlier when they did a cursory check of the vehicle?

He made his way back into the ranch and held it up. "This is how they found us." He threw it on the table. "I can't believe we didn't find it before this. Now it's too late." His voice choked. Had he lost the one woman he'd fallen in love with? Would he get to tell her how he felt?

Murray squeezed his shoulder. "Don't blame yourself, man."

"He's right," Constable Yellowhead said. "They've been one step ahead of us."

"There has to be someone leaking information to them." Layke sat down at the table. "Can't dwell on that now. We need this plan to work."

A knock sounded on the front door.

"I'll get it," Murray said.

Layke jumped up and unleashed his 9 mm. "No! Get in the corner with Natalie. Constable, you're at my flank." Could he trust this officer? Was he the mole? Right now, Layke didn't have a choice. Hannah's and Gabe's lives were at stake. He handed the man the gun he'd brought in from the Jeep.

He checked the chamber. "Got it."

They skulked their way to the front door.

Layke eased his head forward to look out the window, then let out a breath and opened the door.

Corporal Elias Bakker had arrived with a team, including a medic. He held up a sat phone. "Got the military at my beck and call. They have their military helicopter ready to fly at your word."

Thank You, Lord. "Good. Everyone in the dining room."

Elias made introductions as the team sat.

Layke gave Elias the latitude and longitude of the area he needed the search-and-rescue team to scour.

The corporal relayed the coordinates into the phone. "Got it." He clicked off. "Now we wait."

"How long will it take?"

"Not sure. I heard on the way here that the Martells have been seen in the area and they're out for revenge. We need to be prepared for the possibility that we're walking into a war. Let's discuss our plan."

They spent the next twenty minutes formalizing their attack and rescue operation.

Natalie grabbed the phone. "I'm going to call all of our church prayer warriors. We need them on this." She moved into the living room.

Good. *God, we can't do this without You.*

He remembered the promise he'd made earlier.

How had he been so blind all these years? God had been right by his side even though Layke had refused to see Him. He'd been too stubborn to admit defeat and trust in the One he couldn't touch. Not anymore. It was time. He bowed his head. *Father, I surrender my life to You. Totally and completely. No matter what happens. You are in control. You've been with me all through my life. Forgive me for not seeing it before now. Protect Hannah, Gabe and the other boys. Protect our team. Help us to capture this gang without any loss of life.*

Murray grabbed his arm. "You okay?"

He smiled as a peace washed over him. "Just fulfilling a promise I made to God earlier. I surrendered to him."

Murray slapped his back. "Good for you. I'm so glad. I officially welcome you not only into our family, but God's family." He pulled Layke into a bear hug.

The sat phone rang. "Bakker here," Elias said. "What? The road is gone? How is that possible?" A pause. "Contact Search and Rescue. We need that chopper to take us in. Now—and I don't care that it's snowing."

"Speak to me," Layke said.

"Good news and bad news. They found multiple images in this area." He pointed to the map.

"The bad news?"

"The road is gone. I've requested Search and Rescue to take us in by helicopter."

"Will they do that?"

"They will if they know what's good for them." He grabbed the sat phone. "We need to roll, though. We'll meet them here." Once again, he pointed to the map, showing a clearing.

"Let's go," Layke said.

Murray grabbed his hand. "Stay safe, brother. Bring them all home."

"I promise."

He would even if it cost him his own life.

Hannah bolted upward. Too fast. The room spun. Why did her head hurt so much? Where was she? She focused her gaze in the dimly lit space. The small room held twin beds and a dresser. The scent of burning logs lingered in the air, telling her a fireplace was nearby. Gabe slept in a bed beside her. A man with a rifle across his lap sat in a rocking chair in the corner, snoring. She rubbed her head. What had happened at the ranch?

Right. She'd heard screaming and knew the gang had found them. She'd called Layke, but the men stormed into her bedroom and destroyed her phone. They hauled her and Gabe downstairs. She tried to stop them, but they hit her on the head. Hard. That was the last she remembered before waking in this darkened area. Was Layke on his way to rescue them? *Lord, make it so.*

She glanced at the man with the long beard in the corner. Could she get by him with Gabe without being heard? Why hadn't they tied her up? Strange. Perhaps it was a God thing. How could she have doubted His sovereignty? *Forgive me, Lord.*

She eased out of bed. The cool floor tickled her bare feet. They had brought her here without socks? Heartless. At least her flannel pajamas provided warmth.

She gently shook Gabe.

He stirred and she whispered in his ear. "Shh. We need to be quiet."

She helped him sit up. "Can you walk quietly?"

He nodded.

A beacon of light shone under the door, guiding them forward.

Gabe hit his knee on the foot of the bed and yelped.

They stopped. She held her breath. The urge to flee washed over her, but she dug her nails into her palms to curb herself from the flight mode. She composed herself, determination setting in. She would not put Gabe in further harm by being reckless.

The man snorted and slouched farther into the chair.

Some watchdog Broderick hired.

They tiptoed by him and Hannah turned the knob, easing the door open.

Gabe grabbed her hand and headed down the corridor. "I know which way to go."

Of course he did. They were at the kidnapper's ranch. She let him lead her, praying as they went.

They inched down a circular staircase and stopped midway. Angry voices sounded beneath them.

She pulled Gabe behind her. How she wished for her Beretta right now.

"I don't care what they say," the deep voice said. "They won't take over my business."

"The Martells are ruthless. They'll kill us all." The man's rushed speech revealed his anxiousness.

A piercing alarm blared throughout the ranch. "What's that?" another voice asked.

A curse resonated up the stairs. "Someone has breached the front gate. They're here."

"Who?"

"The Martells. They're out for blood. We need to get my wife and everyone else onto the snowmobiles."

Wife? That had to be the woman Gabe talked about.

"What about the kids?"

"Leave them."

What? Hannah gasped. She clamped her hand over her mouth, but it was too late. It had echoed into the hallway.

"Who's that, Broderick?"

The man they'd been hunting was here and she was about to meet him face-to-face.

Footsteps pounded nearby.

"This way." Gabe grabbed her hand and they scurried down the rest of the stairs, turning right at the bottom.

"Stop, little one," the voice boomed.

Impossible! It couldn't be. She skidded to a stop on the hardwood floor and slowly turned.

And gazed into the hardened eyes of her beloved boss.

A cool breeze hovered around her ankles and lingered, slinking up her legs.

"Doyle? You're Broderick?" The room spun, and she braced herself against the wall as dread cemented in her stomach. Thoughts of their relationship scrambled through her mind, betrayal setting in. How could she have been so blind? He deserved an Oscar for fooling her all these years.

"I'm surprised you didn't figure it out sooner. You and that insufferable Constable Jackson."

She rushed at him and pounded her fists on his chest. "How could you? I trusted you."

"I needed the money."

She pulled back. "What? This was all for you to get rich? Didn't the CBSA pay you enough?"

"I have my reasons." He grabbed her arm. "Why did you have to get in the way, little one?"

She yanked herself free. "Don't call me that. You don't have the right." She pushed away the emotion threatening to consume her. "How long have you been smuggling children?"

"Two years and, yes, it was inside fish trucks. I lied about that when you asked me to look into it."

Her jaw dropped. "So, this is how all of those men knew everything about us. Where I lived, where we hid, and every move we made?"

"Yup."

"And you've been holding these children here for two years?" How had he gone unseen for that long?

"Some of them, but then we needed more. That's when we grabbed Gabe and his buddies. Plus Noel's church group."

"Where is Noel?"

"Don't you worry, we have him under control. Now."

She clenched her fists but kept them at her sides. "What did you do to him?"

"Sedation. My men were tired of his screams."

Gabe whimpered in the corner.

Doyle's attention diverted to the boy. He rushed over and hauled him up. "And you... You cost me thousands. We had to destroy the mine because you escaped." He shook him in midair.

"My love, stop!" A voice behind them commanded obedience.

Hannah turned.

A frail woman in her forties stood with a housecoat wrapped around her and a cane at her side.

The lady Gabe spoke about was Jennifer, Doyle's wife? Hannah almost didn't recognize the woman. Apparently, she'd gotten sick and Doyle hadn't brought her around to see anyone for quite some time. "Doyle, why didn't you tell us she was sick? Why hide it?"

"She wouldn't let me," he said.

"I refused to let anyone pity me, so I moved out to this location to get out of the public's eye." Jennifer raised her cane at Doyle. "Let the boy go. This needs to end now."

"Babe, I need you to go back to bed." His softened voice betrayed his feelings for the woman.

If he was capable of having feelings.

"I won't. Not until you promise me you'll stop all this nonsense. You can't save me from this."

Save her from what?

"What's wrong with her?" Hannah asked.

Jennifer stepped closer.

It was then Hannah noticed her pale gray face.

"I have Lupus. A long-term autoimmune disease that has no cure."

Hannah mentally searched the recesses of her mind for more information. The disease affected many people. "I'm sorry you have this. How long ago were you diagnosed?"

"A few years now, but I hid it well until recently. Good to see you again, Hannah."

Jennifer smiled at Gabe. "Hey, Gabe. So glad to see you're safe."

The woman's gentle demeanor struck Hannah. Why hadn't she tried to stop Doyle before this?

"I know what you're thinking, Hannah. Why didn't I stop Doyle sooner? You see, he promised a cure and a family of kids. That gave me hope, so I turned a blind eye until they brought Noel here. He'd gone too far this time. That was when I turned my back and let Gabe escape."

"You what? It was you?" Doyle's gruff voice boomed. His men came running.

"Boss, you okay?"

Doyle held his hand up. "Go secure the perimeter. We can't let the mafia get inside."

The men rushed off with their rifles at the ready.

"Babe, why did you do it? You knew we were getting closer to finding a cure."

Wait? Doyle did all this to fund research for a cure?

"But not at the expense of these poor boys. And we need to get Noel back to his parents." Jennifer turned. "I'll go get him so Hannah can take him home."

Noel! She turned to Doyle. Would it be as easy as Jennifer thought? Hannah knew better and had to talk him down. "You need to let me help him and all the boys. This isn't you. You are kind and noble."

He laughed.

A laugh that chilled her to the bones.

This was *not* the man she knew.

It was then she realized.

She'd never be able to talk him down. Not when his wife still carried this terrible disease. His mission was to find a cure and he obviously wouldn't stop until he found one.

Lord, help us.

A whirling sound broke their silence.

Doyle stiffened and grabbed his radio. "Manny, what's that?"

"Helicopter. Search and Rescue, boss."

Layke! He'd found them.

Doyle pulled out a Glock and aimed it at her. "Don't think your boyfriend is here to save you. He—"

Gunfire broke up his words.

Hannah stiffened as the walls seemed to close in and her chest tightened.

Was that Layke or the Martells?

Layke and his team rappelled down the ropes from the red-and-yellow Search and Rescue helicopter into a small clearing close to the ranch. God had slowed the storm for them and allowed the team to make it to the gang's hideaway in record time. At least, that's what Layke believed. It was the only answer. His feet touched the ground and he immediately raised his MP5 submachine gun.

Gunfire erupted in the distance. Obviously, the mafia had beat them to the location. The muscles in Layke's shoulders tightened. This changed everything. They would now be battling two enemies vying for territory. Not a good combination.

"The Martells are here." Layke motioned the team onward. "Take up your positions, and wait for my signal."

They fanned out.

Layke and Elias moved forward with the medic behind them.

They ran in a crouch sprint format and hid behind the trees in front of the main ranch house. Muzzle shots lit inside the dimmed establishment. The Martells had breached the premises. Was he too late?

A scream pierced the night.

Hannah! He needed to get inside.

He surveyed the outer area of the log ranch and didn't see anyone lurking. They had to move in. He reached for his radio. "Take positions around all exits. Wait for my word to breach. Keep your eyes open. We have both Broderick's men and the Martells fighting over territory. This won't be pretty." He turned to Elias. "Let's go."

They ran up the front stairs onto the veranda, and stood on either side of the door. Layke prayed a desperate prayer before grabbing his radio again. "Breach! Breach!"

Elias opened the screen and kicked in the wooden door.

They skulked inside.

Loud voices drew them down the hall.

Layke motioned for Elias to go right. Layke turned left and moved down a hall before halting at the sight in the enormous living room.

Hannah, Gabe and another woman were huddled in a corner with an assailant pointing a gun in their direction. Layke stared at the back of the dark-haired man. His stance seemed familiar. Where had he'd seen him before?

Other men surrounded the group, angling their rifles at the suspect.

A slender man dressed in a suit stepped forward with henchmen at his side. That had to be Perry Martell.

This was about to get messy. Too many men. Too many guns.

"Give it up, Broderick," Perry said. "Your diamond mining is now closed for business. Let the woman and kids go. You don't need them any longer."

The politician was going to let them go?

The man turned and Layke caught a glimpse of his face. He drew in a sharp breath.

What? Doyle was Broderick?

Layke had never trusted him. Something had always rubbed him the wrong way. Now he knew why. But how had he kept ahead of their every step? He glanced at Hannah just as she looked his way. Her eyes widened.

He raised his finger to his lips, motioning her to be quiet.

She gestured her head toward Doyle.

Layke's other men crashed through the back of the house. More gunfire erupted.

Hannah plowed into Doyle, knocking the gun out of his hand.

Layke rushed into the room. "Police! Stand down."

Perry pivoted and raised his gun.

A shot rang out and the mafia king dropped.

Elias had made his way around and came through a different entrance. He pointed his weapon at the other men. "Don't move. It's over."

Constable Antoine rushed in with his weapon raised, Constable Yellowhead behind him.

Doyle dove for the Glock on the floor. He turned it toward Hannah.

It was like a movie playing in slow motion.

"Gun!" Layke pushed forward and fired, hitting Doyle's arm.

He dropped the weapon and clutched his limb. He let out a cry and grabbed the woman's cane, rushing toward Hannah. "You'll pay for ruining everything."

Layke sprinted across the room, catapulting over chairs into the air and threw himself on top of Doyle.

They crashed to the floor with a thud. Layke's head cracked on the hard surface. White spots sparkled in his vision like stars twinkling in the night.

Doyle moaned in pain.

Hannah rushed over to Layke and pulled him into her arms. "You saved me."

He tried to sit, but the room spun and darkness threatened to pull him under. He fell back down.

"Layke! Stay with me."

He inhaled and counted before exhaling. His vision cleared and he eased himself up. "I'm okay."

Elias pulled Doyle up and shoved him into a chair, aiming his gun at his head. "Move and you'll be sorry."

Doyle sneered and pointed toward the door. "She might have something to say about that."

"Let him go," boomed a menacing voice.

They turned.

Martha Bakker stood with a Glock in her manicured hands.

Hannah bolted to her feet. "Martha, what are you doing?"

"Drop the gun, Elias." Gone was the sweet mother figure everyone in Beaver Creek knew. Or thought they knew.

Elias let his gun fall to the floor. It clunked on the hardwood. "Why, my love? Didn't I give you everything?"

She laughed a heinous laugh.

It sent chills through Hannah's body. How had she been deceived by both Doyle and Martha? Their betrayal reached to her core. How would she ever come back from this?

Then she glanced at Layke. The man she'd fallen for. She had to save him. Save Gabe and the others. But how?

"I fooled you all." She stepped farther into the room, stopping beside Elias. She raised the gun to his head. "Especially you."

"Why?" Elias's whispered question was barely audible.

"My family was right. I never should have married you. I deserved more than just a simple policeman's salary. I had a lifestyle to uphold. Doyle knew I wasn't happy and told me about Jennifer's worsened condition. He shared his plan to make money to find a cure. We came up with my involvement of pretending to work on the books at the detachment to feed them information. No one was the wiser." She rushed over to Gabe. "And then you got away, you brat." She hauled him by the collar.

"No!" Layke yelled before he fell back down.

"Layke?" Had his hit to the head taken over? She had to act.

Gabe whimpered.

Hannah's motherly instinct emerged as a memory flashed before her. Layke's ankle gun!

She dropped to her knees and pulled it out of his holster before whipping it up in Martha's direction. "Stop, Martha! It's over."

"You really think you can save everyone, dear Hannah? You should have died from the poison I'd arranged." She raised her Glock. "But you will now."

Hannah was able to take a shot before Martha could pull the trigger.

The woman fell to the floor.

Elias yelled and rushed over to his dying wife. "Why? Why? Why?" He rocked her in his arms.

Constable Antoine scrambled to where Doyle sat and pulled him from the chair. "You're done." He escorted him out of the room.

Hannah fell beside Layke. "Don't leave me."

A scurry of activity sounded behind her.

A man rushed forward with a bag and squatted by them. "I'm a medic. Let me look." He felt for a pulse. "Good. It's steady."

Relief showered her with hope.

The medic pulled out a light and opened Layke's eyes, shining it in. "Pupils look good. I think the fall knocked him out. Probably a concussion. He'll need to be checked out at a hospital."

"Mr. Layke!" Gabe yelled. "Is he going to be okay, Miss Hannah?"

She pulled the boy into her arms. "God's got this," she said, finally believing in His sovereignty. He wouldn't leave her now. He had a plan for her life. Whether or not it was with Layke, she didn't know. Yes, she couldn't have children, but maybe there were other options. She believed. Her identity in Him once again secured. Forever.

Layke stirred. "Hannah?"

She let go of Gabe and caressed the constable's face. "I'm here."

Constable Yellowhead held out his hand to Gabe. "Son, how about we go find the rest of the boys? Can you show me where they are?"

Gabe jumped up. "Let's go find my friends!"

The medic helped the crying Jennifer up and they shuffled out behind them, leaving the chaotic room in silence.

Layke eased himself into a seated position. "I'm sorry about Doyle. I had no idea he was Broderick."

"He fooled all of us. Martha, too." Hannah scooted herself closer to him. "I was so scared I'd lost you."

"You didn't." He reached up his hand and rubbed her cheek. "How can I leave you when I just found you?"

"Even when you know my condition?"

"Hannah, there's always adoption. I want you in my life."

She snickered. "But you'll hate winter here in the Yukon."

"It will grow on me as long as you're by my side."

Their gaze held. "I could get lost in your ocean-blue eyes," she said.

He cupped his hand at the back of her head and pulled her closer. "I love you, Hannah Morgan."

Her breath hitched as her heart pounded in anticipation of his mouth on hers. She closed her eyes.

His lips met hers in a tender kiss.

They ended their embrace but touched forehead to forehead.

Hannah caressed the stubble on his chin. "I love you, too."

Happy tears welled, warmth spreading throughout her body. God had not only confirmed her identity in Him, but gifted her with a love she'd never dreamt possible.

Until now.

EPILOGUE

One year later

Hannah stood at the back of the church, holding a bouquet of white roses and poinsettias. Her white gown shimmered in the dimly lit room on a cold winter's night. Candles flickered, their illuminating flames dancing shadows on the walls.

Everything was perfect.

Layke stood at the front dressed in his police uniform and looked even more handsome than when she first met him one year ago today. If that was even possible.

Doyle had been found guilty on all charges and was serving life in prison. Both his and the Martells' businesses crumbled. Jennifer now lived in a facility with full-time care. Elias had taken his wife's betrayal and death hard, so when a position opened up at the Whitehorse detachment he transferred.

And Gabe?

He stood at the front at Layke's side.

The adoption papers would go through any day now. He would be their son. God had given her not only the gift of a husband, but a sweet son. She looked forward to a lifetime of building snowmen with them both.

Kaylin Steeves settled into her position beside the group

in her red gown, her diamond and matching wedding band glistening. Their best friends had made the trip to the Yukon to be their witnesses.

Music played softly in the background as she made her way to the front. She caught Layke's gaze. His eyes widened and he winked.

She walked by a row of family. Layke's brother Murray, Natalie and their son, Noel. Layke had put in for a transfer and moved to the Yukon six months ago. In the summer. His favorite season.

Next to Murray's family sat a woman beaming from ear to ear.

Layke's mother. It had taken lots of counseling and letting go, but he'd forgiven her. They now kept in constant contact.

On the other side of the room, her adoptive family smiled. She vowed to herself to stay more involved in their lives even though distance separated them. Life was too short.

She reached the front and Layke stepped forward. "You're beautiful."

"Thank you, my handsome constable."

He leaned in for a kiss.

"Whoa now!" the pastor said. "It's not time for kissing yet."

"Sorry, I couldn't help myself," Layke said.

The crowd chuckled.

"Dearly beloved. We're gathered here today on this cold wintery day to join this man and woman in holy matrimony."

Fifteen minutes later, they walked down the aisle after being pronounced man and wife.

Layke leaned in. "I have a surprise for you."

"What?"

"This." He nodded at Hudson, his best man, and his brother, Murray. They opened the church doors.

A sled sat at the foot of the steps along with Murray's dogs.

It was decorated with a Just Married sign and Christmas garland.

Saje barked, her brown and blue eyes sparkling.

Hannah laughed. "For real?"

"Yes. Your chariot awaits, my love."

The dark sky changed and colors of green, purple and blue shimmered across the area behind the distant tree line.

The crowd gasped at the sight. Stars twinkled as if showing off for the special occasion.

A spectacular display added to her already perfect day. *Thank You, Lord.*

She pulled her husband closer and kissed him.

Her handsome prince.

* * * * *

If you liked this story from Darlene L. Turner,
check out her previous
Love Inspired Suspense book:

Border Breach

Available now from Love Inspired Suspense!
Find more great reads at www.LoveInspired.com.

Dear Reader,

Thank you for taking Layke and Hannah's adventure with me. I enjoyed setting it on the Yukon/Alaskan border for many reasons. I love snow, plaid shirts, mountains and log cabins. Plus, my sweet brother and sister-in-law lived in the Yukon at one point, so I was able to see some amazing scenery while visiting Murray and Natalie. This book is a tribute to him and the legacy he left behind.

I try to incorporate everyday struggles in my stories, so we can see there's hope in what we go through and put trust in our sovereign God. This story is about forgiveness and also being thankful for the way God made us—in His image.

I'd love to hear from you. You can contact me through my website, www.darlenelturner.com, and also sign up for Darlene's Diary newsletter to receive exclusive subscriber giveaways.

God bless,
Darlene L. Turner

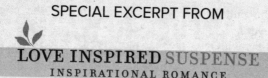
A wedding party is attacked in the Alaskan wilderness. Can a K-9 trooper and his dog keep the bridesmaid safe from the lurking danger?

Read on for a sneak preview of
Alaskan Rescue *by Terri Reed in the new*
Alaska K-9 Unit *series from Love Inspired Suspense.*

A groan echoed in Ariel Potter's ears. Was someone hurt? She needed to help them.

She heard another moan and decided she was the source of the noise. The world seemed to spin. What was happening?

Somewhere in her mind, she realized she was being turned over onto a hard surface. Dull pain pounded the back of her head.

"Miss? Miss?"

A hand on her shoulder brought Ariel out of the foggy state engulfing her. Opening her eyelids proved to be a struggle. Snow fell from the sky. Then a hand shielded her face from the elements.

Her gaze passed across broad shoulders to a very handsome face beneath a helmet. Dark hair peeked out from the edge of the helmet and a pair of goggles hung from his neck. Who was this man?

The pull of sleep was hard to resist. She closed her eyes.

"Stay with me," the man murmured.

His voice coaxed her to do as he instructed, and she forced her eyes open.

Where was she?

Awareness of aches and pains screamed throughout her body, bringing the world into sharp focus. She was flat on her back and her head throbbed.

Ariel started to raise a hand to touch her head, but something was holding her arm down. She tried to sit up, and when she discovered she couldn't, she lifted her head to see why. Straps had been placed across her shoulders, her torso, hips and knees to keep her in place on a rescue basket.

"Hey, now, I need you to concentrate on staying awake."

That deep, rich voice brought her focus back to the moment. Memory flooded her on a wave of terror. The horror of rolling down the side of the cliff, hitting her head, landing in a bramble bush and the fear of moving that would take her plummeting to the bottom of the mountain. She must have gone in and out of consciousness before being rescued. She gasped with realization. "Someone pushed me!"

Don't miss
Alaskan Rescue *by Terri Reed,*
available wherever Love Inspired Suspense
books and ebooks are sold.

LoveInspired.com

LISEXP0321